The First Souvenir

He was standing so close to her that their bodies were almost touching. Unnerved by this, Racile threw up her hands to push him back. For the moment, she had forgotten that he had used his shirt to wipe her face. Now the contact of her hands against the bare skin of his chest was like a shock of static electricity.

Her heart raced and involuntarily her eyes met his. She felt an almost explosive reaction run up her spine. Clay's eyes bored into hers.

The sudden sound of a car horn, honking in a rapid repeating pattern to announce its arrival, caused Clay to trace his fingers caressingly across the arch of her cheekbones. He stepped away from her. "That must be Larry. For a few minutes, there, I forgot completely that he was coming in this morning." His meaningful look was followed by a smile.

FRAN WILSON

is a woman of many talents and interests. She is a published writer of both fiction and nonfiction, has worked as an announcer and news reporter for a radio station, and has written music. She enjoys traveling, collecting Seri Indian wood carvings, and refinishing antique furniture.

Dear Reader:

I'd like to take this opportunity to thank you for all your support and encouragement of Silhouette Romances.

Many of you write in regularly, telling us what you like best about Silhouette, which authors are your favorites. This is a tremendous help to us as we strive to publish the best contemporary romances possible.

All the romances from Silhouette Books are for you, so enjoy this book and the many stories to come.

Karen Solem
Editor-in-Chief
Silhouette Books

FRAN WILSON
Souvenirs

Silhouette *Romance*

Published by Silhouette Books New York

America's Publisher of Contemporary Romance

Other Silhouette Books by Fran Wilson

Where Mountains Wait
Amber Wine
Winter Promise
After Autumn

SILHOUETTE BOOKS, a Division of Simon & Schuster, Inc.
1230 Avenue of the Americas, New York, N.Y. 10020

Copyright © 1983 by Fran Wilson

Distributed by Pocket Books

ISBN: 0-671-57263-6

First Silhouette Books printing December, 1983

10 9 8 7 6 5 4 3 2 1

Map by Ray Lundgren

America's Publisher of Contemporary Romance

Printed in the U.S.A.

BC91

For Tommy,
with all my love,
for the past,
for the present and forever.

Joy and laughter
Recalled through the years,
Dreams turned to memories
Love's souvenirs.

f.e.w.

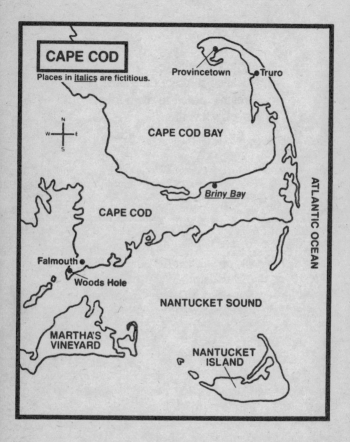

CAPE COD

Places in *italics* are fictitious.

Provincetown • • Truro

N
W — E
S

CAPE COD BAY

Briny Bay

CAPE COD

Falmouth •

Woods Hole

NANTUCKET SOUND

ATLANTIC OCEAN

MARTHA'S VINEYARD

NANTUCKET ISLAND

Chapter One

Perhaps the April rains had ended with the month. At least, on this the first day of May, the skies over the Philadelphia suburbs were cloudless and had the deep blue color of spring hyacinths. Inside her apartment, converted from an 1890 fieldstone carriage house, Racile Douglas was just finishing dressing for the day. She wore a dove gray, tailored suit with a softly feminine white blouse. In this outfit she felt ready for whatever restaurant Burke might choose for lunch, and yet not too dressed up for her morning at the Pennsylvania Wallcovering Company where she worked as design director.

Tying the bow at the neck of her silk blouse, Racile gave a brief thought to her luncheon date with Burke Mitchell. He'd stressed that it was to be a rather special occasion, saying he had something important to discuss with her. The bow didn't look right, the loops were of unequal size. She pulled the two ends and began to redo the tie. Her fingers were clumsy and she realized she was nervous about seeing Burke today. She had known him for over a year now and during the last four months they had seen a great deal of each other. He cared a lot about her; he'd made that fact quite obvious. In fact, if it hadn't been for her mother's illness and recent death, Racile knew Burke would have tried to force her to make a decision about their relationship before now. Somehow she sensed that this was the subject he intended to discuss with her today. She was fond of him, very much so in fact. Certainly she cared more for him than she ever had for any man before. Why then did she feel reluctant to make a commitment to him? She pressed her lips together thoughtfully. She cared about him, but did she truly love him? How could she really know? She ran her fingers under the lapels of her suit jacket, her mind still reeling from unanswered questions. She needed to find some answers, and she needed to find them today.

Leaving the room, Racile moved quickly down the spiral, wrought-iron staircase which took her from the upper, loft-level bedroom to the attractive, country style living area below. Pausing as she reached the last step, she looked toward the front of the house where beams of sunshine now poured through the bay window, making pools of yellow light on the aged pine surface of the antique desk. She breathed a long sigh, her attention drawn to the documents and the jewelers' box, the contents of her mother's safety deposit box, which she had placed on the desk the night before.

She walked across the oval braided rug and sat down at the desk. Placing rubber bands around the legal papers, she locked them in the narrow drawer of the desk. Dusting her hands, she picked up the small, square box, flipping the lid open with her thumb. For the first time since her mother's funeral, she removed the emerald and diamond ring from the velvet-lined box and slipped it on. It fit the third finger of her right hand perfectly. This did not surprise Racile. Her mother had always said that their hands were alike. Racile's hands were graceful with long slender fingers just as her mother's had been. It was only to be expected that a ring made to fit the lovely hand of Madelaine Douglas would also fit that of her daughter.

Racile also resembled her mother in other ways. She had the same heart-shaped face and velvet-soft, ivory complexion; the burnished gold hair that was neither blonde nor chestnut, but a mixture of both and reminiscent of a Titian painting. Racile had wide-set, violet-blue eyes. The color was the same as her mother's, though the expression was vastly different. Racile's bright eyes reflected her eagerness for life. They were eyes that danced with joy, promising laughter while they whispered something tender, because they could tease as well as caress.

Madelaine's expression had not been the same. As long as Racile could remember, she had seen a pensive expression in the depths of her mother's amethyst eyes. It was as though Madelaine had been lost in some distant dream. There had been a wistful sadness there too, and a look of loneliness even before her husband's death. Warm tears wet her lashes as Racile remembered the automobile accident on the rain-slick surface of the turnpike that had taken her father's life three years ago. Racile moved her head sadly from side to side as if to alter the pattern of her thoughts.

Concentrating her attention again on the ring, she held her hand out in front of her. Sunshine pierced the rich green of the emerald and sparkled over the row of diamonds that surrounded the square green stone. It was a magnificent ring. Strange that she had never seen her mother wear it. She had never even known her mother owned such a valuable piece of jewelry. Where had it come from? Who could have given this to her? Certainly not her father; Racile could be sure of that. Ned Douglas had never stayed with one job long enough to earn the kind of salary required to buy a ring as extravagant as this for his wife, much as he might have wanted to. She frowned. How many different jobs had her father tried? Each time he made a change he'd been so sure that this time he was in the right job, the one for which he had all the qualifications and abilities required to advance rapidly to the top. Perhaps, in his last one, he might have made it. But he did not live to find out.

Racile and her mother had been close, but there seemed to be a number of secrets her mother had not shared with her. For besides the ring, there had been another surprise among the contents of the safety deposit box. There was the deed to a house on Cape Cod made out in her mother's name.

What reason could her mother have for owning a piece of land and a house at a place called Briny Bay, Massachusetts? Why, for heaven's sake, hadn't her mother mentioned this to her? The previous night as she looked through the papers the lawyer had given her, Racile had noticed that the date on the property deed was just a little over a year ago. It was the time after Madelaine had discovered she had terminal cancer. Why would she have wanted to obtain a house on the Cape, knowing she was dying? It didn't make sense. For a matter of fact, Racile doubted that her mother could have afforded to buy a house anywhere unless she'd spent all of the insurance money her father had left. However, most of that sum had been invested in a few high yield bonds, and the small remaining amount into a savings account which was still intact. What earthly reason could her mother have had for not telling her about the ring or the house? Her eyes narrowed quizzically. She sensed that there was somehow a connection. Someone had given Madelaine Douglas an enormously expensive ring. Perhaps, that person had also made it possible for her to have the property.

Snapping the empty ring box closed, Racile pushed it to the back of the desk. Certainly, she could not leave a valuable ring lying around the house while she was at work. It had been her mother's, but it was hers now. She had inherited the emerald ring and she would wear it and enjoy it. After all it was a keepsake, a beautiful souvenir from her equally beautiful mother. That was all that really mattered. It was all she needed to know.

Pushing the chair back from the desk, she got up and walked across the living room to the recessed area behind the staircase which served as her studio. Though a small room, it was sunny and full of light. With windows on three sides, it was the most cheerful area of the carriage house. Racile spent most of her time here creating designs for wallpaper because the company allowed her the freedom to work out her own schedule, as long as she spent a few hours at the office in Philadelphia. Removing the new Oriental designs she had completed from her drawing board, she slid them carefully into a large portfolio. Racile was excited about these new designs for she had created wallpaper so that they could be coordinated with other wallcoverings and with fabric to be used in draperies, upholstery, dust ruffles and pillows. Glancing at her watch, she realized that if she left immediately she would have enough time to make the thirty-eight minute drive to Philadelphia and still get into her office at ten as she'd planned.

As she crossed the living room to the front door, the phone rang sharply. She toyed with the idea of ignoring it in order to avoid a further delay. It rang again. It could be Burke calling to tell her where to meet him for lunch. Curiosity got the best of her and she turned toward the desk, lifting the phone just as it started to ring a third time.

"Hello," she said crisply.

"Hello, this is Clayton Forrest out on Cape Cod. Is this Miss Douglas?"

Racile did not recognize either the name or the vital masculine voice which sounded strong enough to be able to project across the miles from Massachusetts to Pennsylvania without the aid of electrical amplification. "Yes, it is."

"The Miss Douglas who acquired the T.J. Hunter house at Briny Bay?"

"Yes, I've inherited a place on Cape Cod. It may be the one you mean." T.J. Hunter. She thought she remembered seeing that name on the deed, but it had meant nothing to her. "It's at Briny Bay." She smiled as she said the quaint, New England name. Of all the romantic sounding villages on the Cape, it was just her luck to be left a house in a town with a prosaic name that sounded almost salty.

"Well, I'm certainly glad I've finally located you. I've been trying to track down the one T.J. deeded his house to for quite awhile. You see, I know that house well and I'm interested in it. Have you listed it with a realtor on the Cape?"

"Listed it?"

"I want to know what real estate office is handling it for you? Tell me, is it one here or are you using some firm in Philadelphia?" He was beginning to sound impatient.

"Neither one," she said tersely.

"Miss Douglas, please. I'm trying to find out what you're asking for the property. I want to buy it and I have to know who will handle the sale for you. Don't you understand?" He spoke slowly, sounding out each word as if he were speaking to a child.

"I understand, Mr. Forrest, but I'm afraid you do not. You see, I really have been much too busy to give any thought to that property. At this point I can't give you a price, because I've made no plans to sell it."

"Of course you're going to sell. Why on earth would someone like you hold on to it," he said scoffingly.

His offensiveness appalled her. What did he mean, someone like her? This man didn't know anything about her. "I simply don't have time to discuss this any further Mr. . . ."

"Forrest, Clay Forrest," he prompted her. "Look, I have an appointment in Philadelphia on Thursday. I think it would be much more pleasant if we could discuss this over lunch." His voice was cajoling and his attitude seemed to have altered abruptly. "Could I take you to lunch on Thursday, say at one o'clock? I assure you I'm prepared to make an attractive offer for your place."

Though it was ridiculous, she was tempted to take him up on his invitation. She was curious about him. She wrinkled her nose. Everybody knows what curiosity did for the cat and it wouldn't do her any good either, she thought. Aloud she said, "I'm sorry. But I'm busy and I'm sure you are too. At this time there's nothing for us to discuss. To tell you the truth, I haven't been to the Cape nor have I seen the house. I don't even know what condition it's in, let alone what I want to do with it."

"I can tell you everything you need to know about it. It's in fairly good shape in spite of the fact that the place has been empty since the owner drowned last summer."

"Oh, I didn't know whether anyone had been living there or not."

"You didn't?" He sounded surprised. "Surely you knew T.J. was living there when he died?"

"Ummm." She made an ambiguous sound, neither affirming nor denying his question. "Last summer was a difficult time," she said thinking of her mother's illness.

"Yeah, I bet it was."

She tightened her fingers around the phone. She detected a trace of sarcasm in his words. "I'm glad to hear the place is in good shape."

"Fairly good, is what I said. The trim needs painting and it probably wouldn't hurt to have someone check the roof and replace some shingles. It's an old saltbox house and over sixty years old."

"You seem to know a great deal about *my* house."

"Well." He laughed for the first time. "I ought to. I have the house next to it. We're close neighbors, Miss Douglas. In fact, you could say we're joint tenants of a sort." He laughed again, but this time there was a caustic edge to his laughter.

"You have me at a disadvantage since you know the place and I don't. But if I own one piece of property and you own the one next to it, how does that make us joint tenants?"

"When I take you to lunch on Thursday we can

17

talk about the many things we have in common. I can promise you that you'll find them most interesting."

"You intrigue me."

"*You* intrigue me, Miss Douglas. It is Miss, you're not married, are you?"

"I . . . well no," she mumbled hesitatingly, wondering what had prompted him to ask that question.

"You don't sound altogether certain about that."

This conversation was becoming absurd. "I am certain, Mr. Forrest. I'm also certain that I'm busy all day Thursday and there's no way I'll be able to have lunch with you. There's no need for us to meet. As I told you before, I'm not ready to discuss selling my property on the Cape. As a matter of fact, I may keep it for some time." She paused and cleared her throat. "Now, you'll have to excuse me because I can't talk any longer. I'm already running late for work."

"All right, if I can't convince you to meet me Thursday, how about coming down to Briny Bay on the weekend? You really should see the place."

"Really, Mr. Forrest. I don't want to be pestered about . . ."

"Look," he interrupted her. "At least promise me you'll let me know when you make up your mind about the house. I do want to buy it when you decide to sell. Don't forget that."

"You've made that quite clear," she said suppressing a smile. He certainly was persistent. She would have to give him that. "Now, goodbye, Mr.

Forrest," she said pointedly, determined to end their conversation.

"Call me Clay, won't you please? And before you hang up, I want to know what M.R. stands for." He swore softly under his breath. "I don't mind telling you I had one devil of a time locating M.R. Douglas. I naturally thought the initials stood for a man's name. How wrong could I be?" He laughed. "Your friend Trenton Hunter hid your identity from everyone. He was as clever about giving his house and possessions to you as he was about plotting one of those intricate, best-selling novels of his. That was quite a maneuver, his deeding it all over to you awhile before he died so that the house wasn't part of his will." There was no laughter behind Clay Forrest's words now.

Racile's head was spinning. What was he telling her? She rocked forward, feeling dizzy and faint. Did he mean that the T.J. Hunter who had deeded his house to her mother was Trenton Hunter, the Pulitzer Prize-winning author? It was inconceivable. She leaned against the front of the desk to steady herself.

"So, tell me what the initials M.R. stand for?" Clay's deep voice prodded her again.

"Madelaine Racile," she said tonelessly, scarcely aware that she was answering him.

"Madelaine . . . lovely name. May I call you that?"

"I go by my middle name, Racile, because . . ."

"Because Racile is interesting and unique," he interrupted her. "I see."

He didn't see, of course, but she was not going to bother to explain. Why should she tell him that her name was the same as her mother's and for that reason she had always been called Racile while her mother was Madelaine. This Clay Forrest was a complete stranger, and a somewhat disagreeable one. He was irritatingly insistent about wanting to acquire her Briny Bay property. Why should she bother to clarify anything for him? He seemed to know a great deal more than she did already. He knew a famous writer had been the one to deed his house to her mother. How could that be? The implication both shocked and astonished her.

Had Clay Forrest ended their conversation or had she? Racile had no idea. Her mind was a jumble of confused thoughts as she hung up the phone, pressing the beige instrument into its cradle. From what Clay Forrest had revealed to her, it was apparent that her mother had known the novelist Trenton Hunter. Undoubtedly she had known him rather well. The famous writer had given her the deed to his house, and it seemed conceivable that he'd also given her the emerald and diamond ring. Absent-mindedly she twisted the ring on her finger. But when? Where? Why hadn't her mother mentioned any of this to her? It couldn't have been a recent relationship or she would have known about it. Racile had never had even the faintest suspicion that her mother might have been involved with a man other than her father. It was going to take some time for her to assimilate this knowledge of her mother's past.

Turning from the phone, she hurried out the front door, locking it behind her. Although Clay Forrest's call was going to make her thirty minutes late, she didn't regret the delay. He certainly had revealed some surprising bits of information about the property she now owned. She was anxious to go to the Cape and discover for herself what there was about the house that made this man so eager to buy it from her. She felt curious about him too, wondering what he looked like, what age he might be. She wished now that she had not been so arbitrary about his invitation. It could be interesting to meet this man who claimed to be a kind of joint tenant with her. As she drove away from the carriage house, she began to consider the possibility of spending the next couple of weeks at Cape Cod.

Burke was already having his first martini when Racile joined him at the table. "I'm sorry to be late." She smiled apologetically. "I got a late start this morning and I've been running behind schedule ever since."

The sandy-haired man stood up and held her chair for her. "Forget it, honey. You're well worth waiting for and incidently, you look beautiful." He brushed his hand across her shoulders affectionately. "Care to join me in a martini?" he asked as he took his seat across the table from her and at the same time signaled to a nearby waiter.

"White wine for me. I've got a design to alter after lunch. I'll need to be able to concentrate without drawing any squiggly lines. Obviously you're not into any important accounting audits this afternoon, if you can indulge in martinis," she teased, wrinkling her nose impishly.

"Don't you remember that I told you today was a special occasion?"

"So you did, and it looks as though you're already celebrating something. What is it?"

"Freedom, freedom from the stagnating routine procedures of the accounting department at Northeastern Steel." He raised both his voice and his glass. "Let's drink to that, Racile."

She lifted her glass, returning his salute. "I'm not certain I understand yet exactly what we're drinking to, but you sound happy about it, whatever it is."

"I gave notice to my boss. After two more weeks Burke Mitchell will no longer be a general accountant hemmed into a dead-end spot in their accounting department." He drained his glass. "What do you think about that?"

She eyed him over the rim of her wine glass. "I'm surprised for one thing. I didn't think you'd been with Northeastern quite two years yet. How can you say you're in a dead-end position? You haven't been there long enough to know that, have you?"

"I've stayed long enough to find out that the opportunities for me are limited—even more limited than they were in my last job."

"Burke, you've had a lot of positions. Maybe, you shouldn't change around so much." A worried frown crossed her face. Burke's attitude about his jobs reminded her of her father.

"Hey, take that frown off your face and for

heaven's sake don't nag me about this. You haven't let me tell you the best part."

"I'm sorry," she murmured. "I'm just surprised about it. I hadn't suspected that you were dissatisfied with your job."

"Well, I am. What I really want to do is go into a public accounting firm and work in the tax department. There's great potential for me in that area." He leaned across the table covering her hand with his. "I've accepted an offer with an accounting firm in Albany, New York. I'm going there the first of next month and I want you to go with me." He pressed her hand firmly. "I need you, honey. We need each other. This job is right for me. I know it is. I can go places with it. Say you'll marry me and come with me."

She felt light-headed and wondered whether it was a reaction to Burke's sudden proposal or because she had drunk the wine on an empty stomach. She was looking at him, but instead of Burke's blue eyes she was seeing her father's gray ones. Was history about to repeat itself? Was she going to do what her mother had done? If she agreed to marry Burke and go with him to Albany, would he, could he, settle down and make a successful life for the two of them? Or was Burke Mitchell a man like Ned Douglas had been? She shook her head sharply as if to clear away the worrisome images.

A tremulous sigh escaped her lips. "My word, Burke. You've certainly laid everything on me all at once . . . a new job, a move to another state. I'm stunned." She had to put him off. "Let's order lunch and talk about all of this," she added quickly. Fortunately at that moment their waiter moved forward offering the menu. She was grateful for the presence of the neatly uniformed man who now hovered silently by their table while they studied the menu. As long as there was a third person to overhear them, Burke could not press on with personal questions.

Racile knew that their relationship had been moving toward a deeper commitment between them, but she hadn't expected anything quite this serious or this immediate. And it had not occurred to her that Burke would ask her to leave Philadelphia. She was doing well in her job and it was important to her. Though they had never discussed it, Racile had a strong suspicion that she made more money at the wallcovering company than Burke did at Northeastern Steel. A look of dismay darkened her éyes. She knew she was a little in love with Burke, and she did not deny that over the past few months her feelings for him had deepened. He was a caring, agreeable man and besides being fun to be with, he was remarkably handsome. Six feet tall with the broad shoulders and hard body of a man used to sports, he looked like the college gridiron hero he'd been six years ago at Penn State. It now seemed apparent that he was still seeking the instant recognition and acclaim he'd had on the football field. The success that had come so easily in those college days with a team behind him to clear the field had not carried through in his career as an accountant.

She hid her face behind the sleek silver and black menu card, relieved that Burke couldn't see her worried expression. Clearly there was only one thing for her to do. She must convince Burke that he needed to get settled in his new work first, and that she had to go to Briny Bay to see what should be done about the property she'd inherited there. After that there would be time for the two of them to talk seriously about their future together.

"Racile . . . Racile, aren't you ready to order yet?"

Startled by Burke's voice breaking into her thoughts, she let the menu slip from her fingers into her lap. Retrieving it quickly, she said, "Yes, yes . . . of course I am." Her eyes grabbed at the first item listed under the luncheon entrees. "I'll . . . I'll have the Denver sole."

Chapter Two

From the map of the East Coast resting on the seat beside her, Racile could see why Cape Cod was called the "strong right arm of Massachusetts." On the map it elbowed out as an odd-shaped bit of land jutting crookedly into the Atlantic from the mainland. Poets had written that the Cape was born of glaciers, shaped at the whim of wind and wave and appeared as a thorn in Neptune's side, a thorn that was a seventy-mile peninsula of moor and marsh, cliff and dune, beach and tidal flat.

She could readily believe every word now as she drove down the peninsula enjoying the sight of low, sculptured sand dunes fringed with beach grass and inhaling the tangy salt air. She followed the famed Cranberry Highway, 6A, for nearly an hour. It seemed to pick up small towns along the way like beads on a string. As she came into Briny Bay, however, she discovered it to be the smallest village yet.

The turn off from the main road which she was seeking was clearly marked. A neat, white, arrow-shaped sign was lettered in black and read, "To Hunter's Ridge." Following the instructions she had been given, she stopped at the house near the turn off where she was to obtain the key to Trenton Hunter's house from a man named John Wharton.

She parked and trudged through the sand to the weathered clapboard house. A ship's bell hung at one side of the door and it made a loud clanging sound as she rang it. Immediately, the door was opened by a middle-aged woman who stared solemnly at Racile, her deep-set, dark eyes magnified by the metal-rimmed glasses she wore.

"I'm Racile Douglas from Philadelphia. I was told to stop here to pick up the key to my house on Hunter's Ridge from Mr. Wharton. I'm the new owner of Trenton Hunter's house there." Racile spoke rapidly, for some reason feeling she needed to explain in detail why she was asking for the house key.

"John's gone to the grist mill over near Stony Brook, but step inside. I'll fetch the key for you." She stepped back from the door so Racile could enter.

The woman walked to the back of the house while Racile waited just inside the front door. A moment later, the older woman returned and handed Racile two keys strung together on a piece of cord that looked like it might have been a section of a heavy boot lace. Tied with the keys was a round cardboard tag on which was printed the name T.J. Hunter.

"I'm eager to see the house," she said inanely, wanting to appear friendly with this woman whom she presumed must be John Wharton's wife.

"It's a nice place. You should find it comfortable." Though she smiled slightly, she still seemed a little standoffish. She had a certain kind of dignity which made her seem calm and a little shy.

"Oh, I know I will." She opened her purse and dropped the keys inside. Before she left, she felt she should bring up the subject of the caretaking fees. It had been eighteen months since Trenton Hunter's sailboat capsized in a storm off Nantucket island. Since he had deeded the house to her mother even before that time, the responsibility of paying John Wharton for looking after the place certainly was now up to her. "Will you tell your husband that I want to pay him what I owe for the care of the house."

Mrs. Wharton shook her head, making her short-cropped salt-and-pepper hair bounce. "Since Mr. Hunter drowned, your neighbor, Mr. Forrest, has paid John to watch after both houses," she stated matter-of-factly. "I don't rightly think that's going to be changed. Least not this year," she added emphatically. "You see, he pays in advance and I guess he didn't know when you might come around to stay at your place."

Racile could feel her face flush. This Clay Forrest acted as if he already owned her house. "Well, I didn't know this, of course. I haven't met Mr. Forrest yet. I assure you, however, that I'll handle everything concerning my property from now on." Her defensive attitude appeared to go unnoticed by the New England woman. At least, she accepted Racile's statement without further comment, merely an assenting nod.

"It was nice meeting you, and if you'll give me the directions I need to get to my house, I'll be on my way." Racile forced herself to smile. "And I'll talk to your husband in a day or two."

Following the directions Mrs. Wharton had given her, she found it took her only about ten minutes to reach the far end of the ridge. Her tires crunched noisily on the narrow, gravel road as she passed a pristine new sign which read PRIVATE PROPERTY—DO NOT ENTER.

As a furor of barking greeted her, she gripped the steering wheel tensely. A strange dog appeared out of nowhere and raced along beside the car, filling the air with sharp, staccato barks. It would seem that Clay Forrest was not the only one who wished to deny her entrance to Hunter's Ridge. Racile stopped her car at the end of the narrow road between two New England-style saltbox houses. The house to the right, situated a few yards away from the road, appeared larger as it had a bigger gable and two tall brick chimneys.

The tan and white collie stood beside her car door, still barking excitedly. Racile leaned her head out the window. "Hello there fellow. Be quiet now. Be a good dog. Quiet now." She tried to make her voice sound firm and confident, but the collie continued challenging her presence and she felt more than a little uncertain about leaving the sanctuary of her car.

"Hush, Rainbow! Come here to me!" The deep, male voice projected clearly, reaching her ears before the tall, broad-shouldered man came into view from around the front of the house.

Against the cerulean blue of the sky, his deeply tanned skin and straight bony features were almost dramatically good-looking. Racile realized that this man must be Clay Forrest. Though she had not actually visualized him before, she thought that he looked as forceful and compelling as his voice sounded. He approached her car.

"Didn't you read the sign? This is private property." He looked at her, his eyes the same tawny brown as his suntanned skin.

"I know it's private. But it is Hunter's Ridge isn't it?" She returned his intent gaze. "You're Clay Forrest, aren't you?"

"That's right." He put both hands on the ledge of her open car window, leaning his face closer to hers. "But I put that sign up to keep aspiring actresses like you from bothering me. I only write the plays, I don't cast them."

Racile blinked at him in openmouthed surprise. "You're a playwright?"

"Bravo . . . bravo!" He applauded with mock enthusiasm. "That was, actually, not too bad. The wide-eyed incredulous look was somewhat overdone, but your tone of voice mirroring astonishment was quite good. Too bad your Thespian efforts are wasted on me. I told you the choice of ingenues is up to the director." His veiled sarcasm was augmented by a look of annoyance that caused angry gold specks to glisten in the depths of his hazel eyes. "Now, why don't you just turn your car around and drive back to where you came from."

"Look." Racile pushed the door handle, opening the car door to get out.

"No, *you* look." Clay pushed the door firmly shut. "You stay right in your car. You may be prettier than the last girl who came out here to get a part in my new musical, but it didn't work for her and it's not going to work for you either. Stop being a nuisance and get off my property!" The commanding tone of his voice alerted the big collie. The dog commenced barking again.

"It's all right, Rainbow. The lady is leaving."

Racile swung the car door open with a determined thrust. "The lady is not leaving." Swinging her shapely legs from under the steering wheel, she sprang lightly from the car. "I'm not an actress and I'm not here because of your play. Fact is . . . I had no idea until a second ago that you were even a playwright." She tilted her head up at him and smiled. "Now after what you've said and the fact that you call your dog Rainbow, I realize you're the Forrest of Forrest and Vernon. Your collie must be the mascot of your latest hit musical, *Rainbow's End.*"

He looked pleased inspite of himself and Racile could see that he was flattered because she knew about his present Broadway success. "You're darn knowledgeable about my partner and me for a girl that's not an aspiring actress." He smiled begrudgingly. "And you're even right about my dog. Larry Vernon gave him to me while the two of us were writing *Rainbow's End*. It seemed only right to name him after the play." His jaw tightened and he frowned, causing the slight smile he'd given her to vanish. "That's enough talk about my play and my pet. Why don't you tell me *who* you are and what you want? Maybe if we can get that over with, you'll get back to where you belong and leave me alone."

"I am where I belong." She laughed and extended her hand. "I'm your new neighbor. I'm Racile Douglas."

His eyes swept over her in rapid appraisal. "I don't believe it. You're too young." His taut expression matched the clipped harshness of his words.

Her laughter died on her lips. "I can't see how my age changes who I am?"

He continued to eye her intently. "I guess it doesn't. However, I had certainly pictured you as someone nearer Trenton's age." His penetrating stare was now fixed on her face. "Did he ever tell you he had a son older than you are?"

She stared back at him without answering.

"I thought not. I'm sorry. Forget I said that." He took a step toward her, reaching now for the hand he'd failed to take when she offered it before. "Your arrival surprised me. I admit I'm disagreeable when someone interrupts my writing." He smiled contritely. "I guess I'm like old Rainbow here. I bark a lot. I seldom bite however." His smile widened revealing straight, even teeth that were startingly white against the deep tan of his skin.

If she had surprised him, he was confusing her. In a split second, his hostile attitude toward her had seemed to vanish, and now he was apologizing to her while pressing her hand firmly and warmly in his. He had been rude before though and she didn't appreciate his insinuations. "You also make wrong assumptions," she countered. If he now wished to clear the air, he'd best be aware of how wrong he'd been. "Without allowing me to explain why I'm here, you first jump to the conclusion that I'm a pushy actress coming to hassle you for a part. Then you question my age as if I were a child. I'm a good deal older than I look," she said, pulling her hand from his. She was suddenly very much aware that he had held her hand longer than necessary for two people who were meeting for the first time. "The way things seem is not always the way things are. Wouldn't you say?"

"I'd say it's still too early to tell."

She nibbled at her lip in irritation. "And what does that mean?"

"Only that I thought I'd solved the mystery of M.R. Douglas when I discovered the initials stood for a woman's name rather than a man's." His eyes combed her face in thoughtful speculation. "Now that I've seen you Racile, I must admit the mystery only deepens."

Something in his manner made her feel defensive and this was not the time to match wits with him. There was enough antagonism in the air between them already. He'd made it blatantly clear that he resented any intrusion on his privacy. She turned to indicate she was leaving. "I'm sorry I interrupted your work, but the road ended rather abruptly here by your house. Besides, I was a little afraid of hitting your dog. He did come awfully close to my car."

Clay put his hand on the dog's collar. "He'll stay out of your way."

"Then is it okay for me to drive closer to the other house?"

"Yeah, swing around my car there." He indicated the jeep which was parked directly ahead of her. "Then angle to the right about two hundred yards. That's as close as you can get and still have room to turn your car around."

She got back into her car while he was talking. Clay closed the door for her. "Roll your windows up when you leave your car. Sudden rainstorms blow by without any warning this time of year."

Nodding her head, she turned the key in the ignition and drove the few hundred yards nearer to the two-story saltbox house situated at the front of the ridge. A flicker of amusement parted her lips in a smile. Imagine the reclusive playwright showing neighborly concern to caution her about the possibility of rainstorms. It would seem he could be affable when he tried.

Racile didn't know what to expect when she stepped inside the traditional old Cape Cod house, but what she found both charmed and excited her. It was pleasant to be greeted with the lemon odor of furniture polish and the less subtle one of floor wax.

She entered the living room walking slowly over the pegged and grooved floors which were partially covered by hooked rugs in muted shades of red, rich deep blues and ivory tan. The room had a comfortable, homey look. Grouped around the fireplace were two Windsor chairs, a fireside pine bench and a deep-cushioned sofa slip covered in a red and blue provincial print. A tavern table was at the back of the sofa and in front of it a teakwood sea chest which served as a coffee table and held an assortment of sea shells, a couple of magazines and a wide-flanged pewter plate which had been an ash tray. The late afternoon light now filtered through the west windows picking up the dull red of the old colonial brick fireplace. A teakettle stand was situated at one side of the brick hearth and it held a pewter teapot. As the last rays of sunlight moved across the surface of the kettle, the pewter gleamed with a rich silver-gray patina. At the opposite end of the room was a grand piano of mellow brown fruitwood. Unconsciously she twisted the emerald ring on her finger. Had her mother ever stood here and gazed around this room as she was doing now? She wondered.

Racile turned around slowly taking in the details of the comfortable room once again. Returning to the small front hall, she picked up her two suitcases from where she'd left them by the front door and started upstairs. Her shoes tapped noisily on the uncarpeted stairs.

She discovered there were three bedrooms on the upper level. One on either side of the stairs and a third, larger one, appeared to spread across the back of the house. This long, rectangular-shaped room had obviously been the one Trenton Hunter used for himself as it was tailored to a man's taste and comfort. A pine, cannonball bed was covered with a red, white and blue woven spread. Along the walls were several bookcases and chests of drawers. In front of the windows a smoking stand stood beside a large leather easy chair with a matching ottoman. Racile did not enter the room, she only stood in the doorway looking in for a few minutes.

One of the smaller bedrooms, the one to the right of the stairs, was the one she chose to use. The soft gray-blue walls had a restful quality, pleasing to the eye. Starched, white, ruffled curtains were tied back at the windows and the four-poster, light cherry wood bed was covered by a white counterpane designed with small figures in blue of the liberty eagle.

When she had unpacked her clothes, she made up the bed using the blue sheets and pillow cases which she found in the blanket chest at the foot of the bed. There were also two blue blankets and a colorful, patterned quilt in the chest. Not knowing just how cold the nights might get here on the Cape even in May, she put all three on the bed before replacing the eagle coverlet.

Knowing she'd made a start at settling in her

new house, she sighed contentedly. Before going back downstairs she took another quick look around. If it was possible to feel curiosity, contentment and excitement at the same time, Racile felt as if she were experiencing all those sensations as she made another tour of the rooms. She was falling in love with a house, this house, her house.

It was getting late and dusk now shadowed the rooms in murky light. Any further explorations would have to wait until she'd eaten some dinner. She also wanted to locate a grocery store in the village and buy coffee and fruit and cereal for breakfast in the morning. She turned on the coach lantern over the front door before she left to drive down to the small section of the beach area that comprised Briny Bay.

It was a quarter of eight when she parked her car near the only restaurant in the village. Facing Cape Cod Bay, it was named The Mermaid Tavern. The entrance resembled the prow of an old sailing ship on which was mounted the well-endowed figure of a shapely mermaid. Inside, the restaurant was neither distinctive nor pretentious, a modest-sized, softly lit room with booths around edges and half a dozen tables filling the center area. As soon as Racile took a seat in a booth near the door, a chubby, blonde waitress in a short blue skirt and a matching middy blouse brought her a glass of water and handed her a well used menu decorated with the picture of a red lobster on the plastic coated cover.

"My it's a small world in Briny Bay isn't it,

Racile?" The male voice had a more pleasant note now than had been evident earlier this afternoon.

She looked up to find Clay Forrest standing by her booth, a faint smile deepening the corners of his mouth. "It would seem to be," she agreed.

He kept looking at her, his eyes warmly appraising, making her wish she'd taken time to redo her makeup before she left the house on the ridge. She was conscious of the rumpled state of her clothes after driving all day in the same blouse and skirt. Clay, on the other hand had changed out of the khakis he'd had on earlier. Now he wore blue slacks with a white knit sport shirt and a blue cardigan sweater. She shifted nervously under his scrutiny and turned her attention back to the menu she held in her hands.

"I see you haven't ordered yet."

"No," she said without looking up at him again. "I just got here."

"Good. I just now came in myself. I'll join you." He slid into the seat opposite her.

Her surprise registered briefly as she pressed her lips together both in irritation and amusement. She didn't know whether to be flattered that he desired her company, or annoyed by his pushy arrogance. He seemed totally confident that she desired his presence in the booth with her. "You don't stand on ceremony, do you?"

"Not often. I find it a boring waste of time, don't you?" He gave her a knowing smile. "Anyway, why should I eat by myself when I can eat with my neighbor?"

"You were demanding your privacy this afternoon and you didn't even want to talk to *your neighbor.*" She eyed him cooly. "Why this sudden change in your attitude?"

"No change," he said, leaning back from the table and crossing his arms across his chest in a relaxed manner. "I want to be alone when I'm writing, but I'm happy to have agreeable companion for my other activities. This afternoon I was writing, tonight I'm not. Not a change of attitude, just a change of activity."

She could feel his eyes on her and it was disconcerting. She pretended to be absorbed in the menu. "If you and I are eating together, let's do it. I'm starved." She steered the conversation to food. "I think I'll have the seafood platter. In a place called The Mermaid that should be the specialty of the house." She handed the menu across to him.

Clay took it but laid it on the table without looking at it. "Good choice. I eat here several times a week and the seafood is very good. Their clam chowder is the best on the Cape, by the way, so I insist you start off with a cup of it."

"You insist on a lot of things, Clay Forrest."

His face sobered. "You don't like clam chowder?"

"I don't like bossy playwrights."

His expression did not alter. "Well, I'm glad it's not the chowder. In New England the witches and those who don't eat clams are burned at the stake."

He maintained his mask of seriousness until she

began to laugh. Then he grinned and signaled the plump blonde girl and gave her their order.

The service was prompt and a few minutes after they had eaten their chowder, their dinner was placed before them. Racile picked up the wedge of lemon on her plate, squeezed it over her fish and began to eat with undisguised relish.

Clay chuckled and she paused, fork in hand, to look at him. "What's funny?" She wrinkled her nose at him. "If you're laughing at me because I'm attacking this fish as if I'm starving, well I am. I haven't had anything to eat since noon today. It's now almost nine o'clock, I'll bet."

He looked at his watch. "It is eight thirty-five to be exact and I'm not really laughing. I'm just relieved to discover you're not a catsup freak."

"What?"

"You used lemon only on your fish. I salute you for that." He lifted his hand to his forehead.

"I'm glad I finally did something that gets your stamp of approval," she quipped and dismissed the subject by taking another bite of fish.

"You haven't mentioned the house," he said. "I imagine you found it dreary and musty after being closed up for so long."

"No, neither one." She shook her head. "In fact, it's such a charming, interesting place, I forgot that it had been empty for several months."

A dark frown creased his forehead, marring his smooth, suntanned features. "How fortunate for you." He paused, cleared his throat and leveled his gaze on her face. She thought she detected some private emotion glistening in his tiger gold eyes. "You should have a comfortable and pleasant weekend here then," he said, ending the look of keen assessment he had been giving her. With a slight shrug, he turned his attention to eating his dinner.

Racile suppressed the urge to tell him that if he thought she was here just for the weekend, he was mistaken. "I understand you've been paying John Wharton to look after both of the houses on the ridge. I want to reimburse you for my share and I'll handle it from here on, of course."

"No need for that. You'll probably put the place up for sale right away and . . ."

Shaking her head, she interrupted him. "I've told you that I have no plans to sell anytime soon. I'm not going to rush into a decision. Certainly, I want to assume all the responsibility for the care of the house."

"We can talk about it later," he said, leaning his head out the side of the booth to get the attention of their waitress. "I'm going to get us some coffee."

"We'll talk about it now, Clay." Her voice was firm and she thrust her chin toward him. She'd had about enough of his high-handed manner. "To tell you the truth, I've never owned a house before. I rather like the feeling of having this one. I may become really attached to it."

He gave her a curious look. "How can you become attached to a place you rarely see? With your life-style, I expect you'll spend a weekend here in the fall and maybe two weeks in the summer and the rest of the time you'll let that house sit idle."

"What gives you that idea? You know nothing at all about my life-style."

"I know you have a job in Philadelphia. You were leaving for work the other morning when I called."

"My job doesn't keep me in Philadelphia. I could work from right here in Briny Bay, if I wanted to."

"How can you do that? What kind of work do you do anyway?" His bemused expression made Racile smile. Clay had such a know-it-all attitude about everything. His preconceived ideas about her were less than flattering. She was going to enjoy proving him wrong on every score.

"I work for a wallcovering company. I'm a design artist." Racile couldn't resist arching a well-shaped eyebrow at Clay and pausing to make a dramatic effect. "I can create my designs for wallpaper wherever I happen to be."

His jaw tightened. He made no comment, but swallowed his coffee, scowling down into his cup.

"I've answered your questions about my work, now how about if you answer a question for me? You keep making remarks about my selling that nice old house. Is it because you're that anxious to buy it, or is there some reason you just don't want me to have it?" She spoke quietly, her eyes intent on his face, wanting to catch every nuance of his reaction to her words.

The powerful line of his jaw was hard and unyielding. "Both."

A tremor of shock raced through her. He

couldn't have said what she thought she heard. "Did you say both?"

He nodded. "You wanted a straight answer. I gave it to you."

"Why? I don't understand." Trying not to become angry with him, she averted her gaze and toyed nervously with the handle of her coffee cup.

"Because, I'm sure you realize, now that you've seen the ridge, that it's a one-owner property. True, they're two houses, but they're close together with no well-defined line to separate them. And one road is shared by both places. That's why it's called Hunter's Ridge, because one person owned it all. Damn it, the old man shouldn't have divided it."

"Evidently he wanted to, otherwise he wouldn't have sold you one house and half the land." She lifted her cup, drinking the remaining coffee and glancing at Clay over the rim.

"Racile I own much more than half. In fact, most of the ridge is in my name. Whether you realize it or not even the road is mine. You can get to your house only by crossing my property." His face was hard, his voice deceptively quiet. "Trenton may have given you his house, complete with all of his furniture and possessions and the lot on which it stands, but every remaining part of Hunter's Ridge he gave to his son."

Her cup almost slipped from her fingers and it clattered sharply as she set it down in its saucer. "You're his son? But . . . but your name is Forrest. . . ." she murmured unevenly.

"My stepfather adopted me so I have his name, Forrest. You see, I was less than two years old when my mother and Trenton were divorced." A twitch of a muscle at the side of his mouth revealed his tension. "But I'll not bore you with the facts of my boyhood."

"I'm not bored, I'm interested. I didn't know that Trenton Hunter had a son."

"Of course you didn't. The great man was not about to tell you he had a son who was thirty-four." Clay's lips curled in scorn. "That makes me at least twelve years older than the girl my father was involved with. So involved in fact that he deeded his house to her before he died, thus it was not part of his will where her right to have it might be contested."

His sarcasm was stinging and the hostility of his words filled Racile with anger. "Ten," she bit the word off. "You're ten years older than I am Clay, just to clear up one of your several misconceptions about me." Pressing her napkin against her trembling lips, she took a deep breath. She could feel the heat rising in her face. Was it her age that bothered him so, or her having the deed to his father's house? Should she explain about her mother? She stiffened defiantly. She had no intention of allowing this overbearing playwright to censure Madelaine. Let him think what he liked. She certainly did not owe this narrow-minded man any explanations of how she happened to have his father's house. Laying her napkin on the table, she slid out of the booth.

"I think we've covered the subject of your age and mine. The point is we're both adults. What do you say we *act* like it?" She turned her back and walked away from him. At the door to the restaurant, she hesitated, remembering that she hadn't paid for her dinner. Without looking back at him, she shrugged and walked out the door smiling. It would serve Clay right to get stuck with her check.

Chapter Three

It was a short distance from the restaurant to the water's edge. The moonlight made a soft, silver path across the sand. As Racile walked along, she found that the low mash of the surf and the long, dying hiss of the foam on the sand was a soothing sound. She welcomed this calming effect on her emotional state.

"Racile . . . Racile, wait."

Hearing Clay's voice, she stopped walking and shuffled her feet back and forth to make brush marks in the deep sand.

Catching up to her, he put his hand on her arm. "At this time of night it's better if I walk on the beach with you."

"Are you asking if I want you to come along or telling me that you're going to?" Clay made no move to take his hand from her arm and she found the light pressure of his fingers warmly pleasant.

"You already know I'm not one to stand on ceremony." He looked down and smiled at her. "And besides this is my favorite stretch of beach. I walk here a lot of evenings when the day's writing hasn't gone well. Helps me untangle a scene when it has to be rewritten."

She drew her arm away and began walking again. She was relieved that Clay didn't probe her reasons for leaving The Mermaid before him. The subject of his playwriting would be a safer subject between them. Obviously he brought it up for exactly that reason. "I know I interrupted you when I drove in this afternoon. I hope I didn't mess up your day's writing."

"It didn't help. You're not just the ordinary run-of-the-mill distraction, Racile." He walked close beside her so that his arm brushed gently against hers.

"And you're not the ordinary run-of-the-mill playwright," she retorted glibly. *Rainbow's End* is *the* smash musical on Broadway and has been for the past couple of years, hasn't it?"

"It's had a great run, you're right, but it closed last weekend. The producers decided not to try to replace the lead and Sylvia Sontag is leaving for the West Coast to star in the film version."

She glanced up at him. "They're going to make a movie of *Rainbow's End?* That's wonderful. You must be excited about that."

"Yeah, I am." He sounded pleased. He put his arm through hers and took her hand, interlacing his broad fingers with her slender ones. "Your hand is small and cold," he commented, squeezing her fingers gently.

The wind had increased and now the gusts blowing off the water felt cold and damp against her skin. Racile shivered. Dressed only in a cotton skirt and shirt, she was not protected from the chilling blasts of sea air.

"Hey, you're getting cold." Clay stopped abruptly and pulled off his blue sweater. "Wear this." He put it around her shoulders, then turned her so she was facing him and tied the two sleeves together in a loose knot across her breasts. "That makes a regular straightjacket," he said, taking hold of her shoulders and looking into her face. His eyes met hers and held them. There was a moment of awareness between them. Racile felt a sudden warmth and it was more than the protection of the sweater he had wrapped around her. The quickening of her heartbeat took her breath away as he continued to contemplate her upturned face.

"What lies beneath that bone-deep beauty of yours?"

He was so close his breath feathered her cheek. Racile knew she should move back away from him, but somehow she lacked the will to try. As if he sensed what was in her mind, he increased the pressure of his hands on her shoulders.

"I'm going to find out, you can count on it." A quiver of emotion ran over his lean, clean-shaven face. He leaned even closer, his eyes like the lens of a camera recording every feature of her face. "And when I do, don't be surprised if I write a play about you." He brushed his lips across hers, lightly, quickly. It was not a kiss, merely a brief touch of his mouth to hers. His unexpected action astonished her, and her own reaction to him astonished her even more. She experienced a sense of regret that his caress had been so fleeting.

Then, just as abruptly as he had kissed her, he placed one arm around her waist and they walked back.

As she drove from the restaurant out to Hunter's Ridge, she kept glancing in her rearview mirror to see if Clay's jeep might be following her. It was not. There seemed to be many different sides to Clay Forrest's personality. He was a complicated man and she didn't know quite what to make of him. Each time she talked to him his attitude toward her seemed to vary. Learning that he was Trenton Hunter's son had surprised her, but it also helped explain his resentment of her. She put her foot on the brake, slowing down to turn onto the ridge road. Remembering the way Clay had looked at her when he put his sweater around her, she smiled. He hadn't seemed to resent her at that moment. She couldn't define the emotion she'd seen in Clay's eyes, but she'd felt stirred by it. She'd been sorry when it had passed.

The following morning she awakened early, ate her breakfast and made a thorough inspection of the exterior of the house in the daylight. Satisfied that Clay had been right when he'd told her the trim on the house needed painting, she added paint to the list of things she wanted from the village.

As she walked around to the back of the house where she'd left her car, Rainbow came bounding across the ridge to join her. The big collie did not bark this morning, but greeted her with vigorous tail-wagging. Obviously Rainbow no longer regarded her as an unwelcome stranger. He appeared to accept her right to be here on Hunter's Ridge even if his master did not. The dog acted as though he'd like to jump in her car and accompany her. She guessed that Clay must have shut him out of the house so he could work at his writing undisturbed.

"You're lonely, aren't you?" She patted the dog's head. "Wait until I get back and you can keep me company while I paint."

As if he understood her words completely, Rainbow watched until she'd started the car, then he picked a spot between her house and Clay's and lay down facing the road to wait for her return.

An hour and a half later, Racile was back, sitting on the doorstep. She had donned a pair of faded, cut-off jeans and a yellow cotton tee-shirt and was methodically stirring the contents of a can of paint. She hummed softly to herself, pleased because she'd managed to get the exact color she wanted for the front door and the window trim of the saltbox house. It was a rust-red that would compliment and give life to the weathered gray wood siding of the house; it was the same shade of red as the old colonial-style bricks used in the two chimneys. Perhaps if she were a conservative New Englander, she might have stayed with conventional white for the trim, but she rejected that as unimaginative. To her artist's eye, this was the perfect color; this was precisely what she wanted for her house. She hummed a bit louder.

"Is that the color I think it is?"

Racile looked around to find Clay standing in front of the house, hands on his hips, and a scowl on his face as he surveyed the front door Racile had just finished painting.

"It is if you think it's an earthy rust-red." Ignoring his displeased look, she gave him her most disarming smile.

"I don't know about the earth and the rust, but it's red all right."

"Goes perfectly with the gray siding. I like it!" Her tone was enthusiastic. She stepped back from the door to give herself a better perspective.

"A red door and white windows, I don't know about that."

"Neither do I. That's why I'm doing the windows rust-red too."

"You've got to be kidding." He walked over to her and looked at her closely. "Nope," he shook his head. "You're not kidding."

She laughed at his exasperated tone. "Don't worry. The effect will be marvelous. I'm an artist. Trust me."

"Whether you're an artist or not has nothing to do with it. These two houses on Hunter's Ridge have always been painted exactly alike."

"Now they'll be different then, won't they."

The angle of her head emphasized the stubborn thrust of her chin. "Unless you'd be interested in having this same color mixed for you. I'd be glad to help you get it right."

"No thanks," he said angrily. "I can't understand why you're doing a pointless job like this anyway. If you waste your whole weekend painting, you'll end up seeing nothing of the Cape."

She picked up the bucket of paint and moved over to one of the front windows. "I don't happen to feel it's pointless and I'll have plenty of time to go sightseeing later on. I'm not here merely for the weekend." As she spoke, she filled her brush with paint and began to work at the top of the window frame.

"Good. So you're taking a few days vacation. All the more reason to relax and enjoy yourself."

She knew he didn't really think it was good. She would be willing to bet that he'd like nothing better than for her to leave and never come back. Wishing he'd go away and get back to his writing, she leaned over to fill her brush with paint again, making no further attempt to carry on a conversation with him.

"Stop messing with that paint and be reasonable." Clay had followed her to the window and as he spoke he grabbed hold of her right arm. His fingers bit cruelly into the soft flesh of her bare arm.

Racile gave a sharp cry of pain, letting the paint brush drop from her hand. It fell with a plop into the bucket, splashing some of the batter-thick liquid back up in her face. "You idiot! Look what you made me do." Instantaneously, she closed her eyes in a self-protective reflex action. In panic she clawed at her face trying to rid her nose and mouth of the acrid smelling paint.

"Don't move. Let me take care of this," he ordered. "You've got paint in your hair and it shouldn't get into your eyes. Keep 'em closed until I can wipe it all off."

"You just leave me alone. Haven't you done enough to torment me today?" she screamed. Her hands felt slimy from the latex paint. She rubbed her palms down the sides of her jeans impatiently.

"Stop yelling and just stand still and allow me to help you." Clay began to wipe her face gently with a soft cloth. It felt strangely warm as he rubbed it over her skin.

"What's that your wiping me with?" she asked, curiously.

"My shirt."

"You took off your shirt to use on my face?"

"I had no other choice." He laughed. "I could hardly strip your tee-shirt off of you now could I? Although I admit I would have found that most interesting." He must have brought his face closer to hers for she felt his warm breath fan her cheek as he laughed again. "Yes, I must say that would have been most interesting." He teased her with his innuendos.

"May I open my eyes now?" she demanded, pretending to ignore his suggestive remarks.

"In just a second. I think the worst is off now."

"Well, it should be. It's taken you long enough." Putting her hands to her face, she wrinkled her nose. "My nose stings and my skin feels like a sticky rubber ball."

"Let me check and make sure I got it all off your lashes." He cupped her face in his hands, lifting her chin so he could look down into her face.

He was standing so close to her that their bodies were almost touching. Unnerved by this, Racile threw up her hands to push him back. She had forgotten about his using his shirt to wipe her face. The contact of her hands against the bare skin of his chest was like a shock of static electricity.

Her heart raced and involuntarily her eyes met his. She felt an almost explosive reaction run up her spine. Clay's eyes bore into hers and she felt herself embraced by his magnetic gaze.

The sudden sound of a car horn, honking in a rapid repetitive pattern to announce its arrival, caused Clay to trace his fingers caressingly across the arch of her cheek bones and then step away from her. "That must be Larry. For a few minutes, I forgot completely that he was coming in this morning." His meaningful look was followed by a smile. "Come on. Let's go meet him." He took her hand to pull her along with him. Rainbow was already racing toward the road, barking furiously.

"I don't want anyone to see me looking like this." Racile balked, looking down at her paint-spattered jeans. "I'm a total mess. I bet I've got rust paint in my hair."

"Don't worry. Larry won't even notice. That guy neither sees nor hears much of anything unless it's set to music." Clay put his arm around her shoulders, leading her toward the road. "He came down to bring the music he's working on for the new play we want to write."

Twisting frantically, she pulled away from Clay. "I don't want to meet a celebrity like Larry Vernon looking like this. You've got to give me time to wash the paint out of my hair and get cleaned up," she said, backing off. "Bring him over later, after lunch."

"Clay, surprise darling!" A stunning blonde woman wearing a marine blue skirt topped with an immaculate white blazer, rounded the corner of the house. "I was crushed when you didn't come to New York for the closing night of *Rainbow's End*. Truly, you broke my heart. So, I simply had to persuade Larry to bring me along today. I do miss you when you hide up here for so long." This cascade of words poured melodically from the softly pouting mouth of the beautiful actress. With her arms outstretched to Clay, she hurried to him, and held her lovely face up to receive his welcoming kiss.

Whirling around, Racile fled into the house. There was no way that she was going to stay and suffer the embarrassment of meeting these Broadway luminaries when she was in such a deplorable state. Especially since Clay's collaborator had brought the incomparable star of their last play to Briny Bay with him.

A few hours later, Clay called Racile, asking if he could bring Sylvia Sontag over to her house to meet her. By this time, Racile had bathed, washed and dried her hair and dressed carefully. She wore a leaf green shirtwaist dress with a belted waistline which showed off her slender figure and a semi-full skirt which accented the grace of her movements as she walked. She might not be able to compete with the striking appearance of the well-known actress, but she was going to give it her best try.

Racile had thought that the incandescence of Sylvia's beauty as seen on the stage was a result of theater makeup and effective stage lighting. Now, however, seeing her face to face, Racile had to admit the star's monumental beauty was the same offstage as on. Clay made the introductions and Sylvia's smoke-gray eyes slanted in a gracious manner.

"Thank goodness for someone nice like you to talk to while Clay and Larry do their thing with words and music at the piano," she said, as soon as Clay left the two of them alone. "Those two men are impossible to be around when they're starting a new play. Clay is unusually aggravating about this one. He refuses to tell me anything at all about it. I was ready to murder him before he escaped my wrath by bringing me over here to visit with you."

Racile was amused by Sylvia's overly dramatic statements, but she carefully refrained from showing it. Instead, she nodded as if she sympathized with the actress.

"You and I will ignore them and I'll fix us some coffee," she said, leading Sylvia through the dining room to the kitchen. "And, I wanted to tell you that I saw you in *Rainbow's End*. You were terrific."

Sylvia looked pleased. "It was a good show. In

some ways I'm almost sorry to see the long run end."

Racile measured coffee into the percolator and plugged it in. "Clay tells me you're going to star in the movie version."

She nodded. "Matter of fact, I'm going to Hollywood the first of the week to sign the contract. That's the main reason I insisted that Larry bring me up to the Cape today. I want to make certain Clay is going with me next week. He can be so obstinate at times." Sylvia had been standing watching Racile take flower-patterned china cups and saucers from the cupboard above the sink. Now she took a seat at the round oak table in the corner of the kitchen by the window. "He's a stubborn guy."

"I know what you mean," Racile agreed. "I met him only yesterday and so far he's objected to everything I've done."

"That's because you're doing it in Trenton's house. You can't imagine how curious he's been to discover whom his father left his house to." She tapped her chin with the tip of a laquered fingernail. "I bet it shook him up to discover it was you."

"He did act a little surprised."

"You had to be very important to Trenton Hunter for him to want you to have this house. He would have left it to his son otherwise." She placed two perfectly manicured fingers against her chin, watching Racile thoughtfully. "Clay can accept that fact. And has, I'm sure. What must bother him is that you knew his father so well.

Clay never had the opportunity to really know him at all."

"Because his parents divorced?"

"Yes, and because his mother saw to it that Clay saw nothing of his real father while he was growing up. It wasn't until after the success of his first play that Clay finally made contact with Trenton. They got together as writers then and they were just beginning to know each other when Trenton drowned."

Racile was placing a cup of coffee on the table for Sylvia. Involuntarily her fingers tightened and she set it down awkwardly. A small amount of the brown liquid sloshed over into the saucer. "Oh, I'm sorry," she said, pushing that cup aside for herself and turning away to pour another for the actress. Her mind was not on what she was doing. She thought of her mother's death. Sympathy for Clay welled in her mind. She knew the grief of losing a parent. At least, she had the comfort of knowing how close she and her mother had been all her life. Clay had been cheated out of sharing anything with his father. And now he didn't even have his own father's possessions. She did. She pressed her lips together grimly. No wonder Clay resented her.

Putting cream and sugar on the table, Racile took a chair across from Sylvia. It struck her that Sylvia must be well acquainted with Clay for him to have revealed his feelings about his father to her. She was the star of his play, of course. Did she play the leading feminine role in his personal life as well? Racile recalled Sylvia's arrival, the rush of endearing words, how she had expected

Clay to kiss her. She'd thought that was merely the familiarity of show business people greeting each other. Now she wasn't too sure and, strangely, it mattered to her to know the extent of the relationship between Clay and this glamorous, self-assured actress.

"You must have known Clay a long time," she said without looking directly at Sylvia. She stirred a scant teaspoon of sugar into her coffee.

"We do go back a long way." She sighed. "I had the lead in his first play on Broadway. You could even say we both started out together. Because it was my first leading part and in his first produced play." Her generous, neatly glossed lips parted as she smiled. "He and I have been mutually good for each other. I've now starred in three of his plays and each one has been a bigger hit than the one before." Reaching for her cup she lifted it to her mouth and sipped the coffee.

"No one could argue with that kind of success."

"And that's another reason why he has to do the screenplay of *Rainbow's End*. I want it to be *my* movie and Clay knows that." She underlined her words with a determined toss of her head. "He can gear the screen adaptation to fit me like a glove. I won't have it any other way." The feminine sweetness had vanished from her voice, replaced by a tone of ruthless determination. That Sylvia Sontag was a self-seeking, ambitious lady, there could be no possible doubt. She was now looking for recognition as an actress beyond the Broadway stage; she wanted to make certain she was acclaimed as a movie personality as well. Could Clay provide this for her? She expected him to. And what else did this beautiful woman expect Clay to provide for her?

Racile jumped up from her chair to get more coffee. She'd had enough of this conversation. The truth was, she'd had all she could take of Sylvia as well. She unplugged the coffee pot and carried it to the table to refill both of their cups. As she tilted the spout over the cup, she caught sight of the green emerald on her right hand. Green was the color attributed to jealousy. Was she jealous of the possible intimate relationship between Sylvia and Clay? Of course she wasn't. The thought was absurd. She didn't care about Clay. She scarcely knew him. She couldn't be interested in him. Wasn't she was more or less in love with Burke? She caught her breath in an audible gasp. Since she'd arrived in Briny Bay yesterday, she had not thought of Burke Mitchell even once until this moment. And Clay Forrest, how many times had she thought about him? Turning her back to the table she took the pot back to the kitchen, setting it at the side of the kitchen counter. With her back still turned, she nervously adjusted her belt and smoothed her skirt as she tried to control her disquieting thoughts. The truth was, since she first saw him, the image of Trenton Hunter's son had never left her mind.

Chapter Four

At five o'clock, Sylvia insisted that she and Racile go over to Clay's and make the men quit working for the day. They let themselves in quietly and stood in the doorway where they could hear the sound of Larry at the piano, but the two men were unaware of their presence. Racile could not resist stepping just inside the room. She could see Clay leaning against the piano, a frown of concentration on his face as he listened to the melody Larry was playing.

"Let me hear the last eight bars again," Clay said, making a notation on the copy of the music score he had in front of him. As Larry obligingly played the line of melody with his right hand, Clay mouthed the lyrics in a quiet monotone.

Then Larry played the portion of the song a second time, now using both hands so the full, rich tone of the music sang through the room. Sylvia walked to the piano to stand behind Larry, resting her hands lightly on his shoulders.

"That's beautiful," she said when he finished. "It's the major song for your new play isn't it?"

Larry nodded his dark head without looking up from the keyboard. His long-fingered hands remained hovering over the keyboard as if he were going to play again. The next minute, however, he flexed his fingers and leaning back away from the keys, he put his hands on his knees. "It's not entirely ready for an audience as yet."

"Whether it is or not, still it's a marvelous melody and I want to be the one to sing it, of course." She put both of her lovely hands now on his shoulders and rested her chin on top of his dark wavy hair as she peered at the musical score on the piano rack. "You have the range too high." She scolded. "If only you'd learn to write your music in my best key in the beginning then it wouldn't have to be transposed for my voice."

At Sylvia's words Larry and Clay exchanged a guarded look. Racile stood a short distance back from the piano where she was observing the interaction between them. Whether the two men realized it or not, their faces clearly gave them away. They had no intention of letting Sylvia sing the songs in their new play. Why was that? she wondered. Sylvia had starred in each of the Forrest-Vernon musicals before. Why not this one? As if that particular thought had now come to Sylvia's mind, she moved away from Larry and walked over to loop her arm through Clay's.

"Well, you two needn't be in such a big hurry to

finish this play anyway. It can't go into rehearsal until the movie of *Rainbow's End* is made and we're all back in New York." Arching her head proudly, she parted her lips in what would be labeled a Sylvia Sontag dazzling smile. "Then my darlings, the perfect combination of the three of us will make your new play a triumph of next season, won't we?" Apparently Sylvia's question was rhetorical for she didn't pause to allow Clay or Larry to make any kind of answer. Tugging at Clay's arm, she pulled him away from the piano. "Come on. Let's break out the ice and fix drinks for everyone. Then you two men can take Racile and me out to dinner."

"That's exactly what we had in mind. We exist to please the ladies, eh Larry?" Clay said brightly and with a smile toward Racile, he added, "there's a restaurant near Wellfleet that serves a hearty bowl of clam chowder."

Racile wanted to demur, but Clay and Sylvia were already out of the room. She moved closer to the piano to ask Larry some questions about the music he had written. She wanted to tell him how much she liked the lovely melody he had just played and ask him if he would play it again for her.

As if he anticipated her request and wished to avoid any further discussion of his songs for the new play, he quickly closed the cover over the keyboard and stood up. "Sylvia is dauntless, isn't she?" He laughed as he said it, yet he didn't smile. "Her self-assurance is also intimidating until you get used to it."

Feeling that he didn't really expect her to

comment on Sylvia's attitude about her career, Racile gave him a noncommittal smile and remained silent. It was the first time they had really faced each other and she took note of the fact that his well-defined features were too sharp to be handsome, but he had compelling deep brown eyes and a head of dark, curly hair. She thought of a few minutes earlier when Sylvia stood behind Larry at the piano, her radiant silver blondness a sharp contrast to his chocolate brown hair and swarthy complexion. They looked fine together, even complemented each other. At this thought, she flushed and looked away. Why was she picturing Sylvia and Larry as a couple? Was it because it bothered her to think of the actress linked with Clay? She toyed with a strand of her hair, twisting it around her finger. Wishing she hadn't come over to Clay's house with Sylvia, she tried to think of some excuse so she could leave.

"You know, it's nice of all of you to include me, but I really can't go out to dinner tonight. In fact, I really must get back to my house now."

"Don't say that. I know you can stay and have a drink at least." Larry gathered up his music and left the piano.

Racile shook her head. "I'm expecting a call from Philadelphia. I shouldn't have left my house at all. Please, make my excuses to the others." Glancing at him, she hoped her reasons for leaving sounded convincing.

"I'd like to twist your arm, if it would do any good." Larry's warm gaze searched her face. "But it wouldn't, I can see that." He shrugged seeming disappointed. "Will you then promise to have dinner with me the next time I come to work with Clay?"

"If you like." She smiled, then started to walk from the room.

"I like," he said. "I'll consider it a date."

Sylvia and Larry left Briny Bay Sunday night and the following day Clay drove to Boston to catch a plane for Los Angeles. Before he left he asked Racile if she minded feeding Rainbow while he was gone. "If you need to leave Briny Bay, go back to Philadelphia, just tell John Wharton. He's accustomed to putting out food and fresh water for Rainbow when I'm away."

She had no intention of going back to Philadelphia, at least not for another couple of weeks. And too, she welcomed the company of the big collie. So she waved Clay off without asking when he might return. His absence from the ridge was no concern of hers. Even so, once Clay's jeep was out of sight, she felt the stillness of the air and the silence that surrounded her. Looking up at the gulls wheeling overhead, she saw the graceful movements of their wings but heard nothing. This morning the sea gulls didn't cry to each other as they headed out over the bay.

Through the week that followed, Rainbow took up his residence at Racile's. When she was outside the dog stayed near her, and at night he slept in the front hall or outside the front door.

John Wharton spent three mornings replacing damaged shingles on the roof. While he had his tall ladder leaning against the house, Racile used it to paint the trim of the second-story windows.

By the end of the week she had all the upstairs windows completed and about one-third of the ones on the lower level. The addition of the rich red paint gave the old house a definite face-lift. She was admiring her handiwork when John Wharton came down off the roof, having finished with the shingles.

"You've certainly got the place looking smart miss," he said rubbing the back of his gray head with the flat of his hand. Then cocking his head at her he grinned. "That flame color gives this old place some zip." Chuckling, he picked up the ladder and carried it out to his pickup truck.

Every evening after dinner, Racile allowed Rainbow to join her in the living room. While he lay on the rug with his head resting on his front paws, watching her through sleep-narrowed eyes, she sat curled up at one end of the sofa reading one of Trenton Hunter's novels. She was consumed with curiosity about the man who'd given this house to her mother and she intended to learn all she could about him. An author often revealed himself through his writing, and by reading Hunter's books carefully she hoped to get an impression of him, an impression that would fit into a pattern that could include her mother. She did not know how many novels Clay's father had written, but she had located eleven stacked on one of the bookshelves in his bedroom upstairs. Quite systematically, she had begun to read them.

She had finished reading one of his earlier novels before going to bed the previous night. Having finished her supper and cleaned up the kitchen, she now went upstairs to select a new book. Glancing at the various titles, she decided to take several downstairs and stack them on the sea chest in front of the sofa. She could decide later in what order she would read them.

The books were wedged snugly together. When she pulled three from the shelf several others fell out on the floor. This made a wide gap and the remaining books slapped down noisily onto the hard wood of the shelf. As she started to straighten them and replace the books that had tumbled to the floor, she discovered an envelope on the shelf. She had not seen it earlier because it had been covered up by Trenton Hunter's novels.

Picking it up, she saw a few words written lightly across the front of it. "Save my souvenirs for me." At the sight of her mother's slanted handwriting, Racile's eye blurred with a sudden wave of emotion. Clutching the envelope against her breast, she hurried from the room, seeking the sanctuary of her own bedroom before looking at the contents of the envelope her mother had marked for safekeeping.

She snapped the wall switch for the overhead light, filling the small room with a soft yellow glow. Sitting down on the edge of the bed, she looked at the writing once more before turning the envelope over and opening the flap. She didn't know what she had expected to be inside, but certainly something other than these few odd scraps of paper. One by one she picked them up to study them closely. There was a portion of a ticket for the ferry from Woods Hole to Martha's Vineyard. The date punched on the stub was June 20, 1967. She stared at it, surprised at its age. She laid it aside and fingered a piece of cardboard, the size and shape of a playing card. It was not from a deck of cards however, but rather a fortune-telling card of the type that comes from a penny arcade or a gypsy's booth at a traveling carnival. The printed message read: "Seek a memento, a token of remembrance as to a place, a person or an experience."

She stopped in her investigation long enough to pull the spread from the bed pillows and prop the pillows against the headboard so she could lean back against them for support. Tucking her feet under her, she ruffled through the remaining assortment of trivia. There was a matchbook cover from the Bass River Rod and Gun Club, a notice of a clambake at Sandy Neck Beach and an address card of an artist who carves birds and mounts them on pieces of driftwood at the crafts shop at East Sandwich. Racile thought of the carved and painted red-winged blackbird mounted on a sun-bleached piece of rough driftwood which she'd seen on the mantel over the fireplace in the living room. She wondered if perhaps Trenton Hunter had purchased this at a time when her mother had been with him.

The final paper appeared to be a receipt or a copy of an order to a jeweler for engraving . . . script, one name . . . Madelaine . . . have ready 7-31-67. Racile eased the emerald ring from her finger, holding it up so she could see inside. In delicate script was engraved her mother's name—Madelaine—nothing more.

June and July in 1967. She tried to recall that summer. Replacing her mother's emerald ring on her finger, she thought, that was the summer she was eight. She'd spent June, July and almost all of August in Michigan with her grandparents. She remembered it now. It had been the longest time she'd ever been apart from her mother and father. That was because her father had changed jobs again, which meant they'd had to move to another house in another city. Her mother had been upset. She remembered now that her mother and father had argued a lot and then her grandfather had come and she'd driven back to Michigan with him. During that entire summer she had believed that her mother had gone to the new town where her father's job had taken him and that the two of them were busy finding a house and getting moved. It would seem however that Madelaine Douglas had spent part of that summer on Cape Cod. And much of the time she'd been in the company of Trenton Hunter. What had happened to bring the two of them together? Absently Racile twisted the ring on her finger. Had their relationship ended with the end of summer? She resolutely gathered up the small pieces of paper and returned them to the envelope. No matter how much she speculated, she would probably never know what part this well-known writer had played in her mother's life. It was just as well. If Madelaine had wanted her daughter to know, surely she would have told her.

She got off the bed and as she left the bedroom she heard the simultaneous sounds of knocking at the front door and Rainbow's short yapping barks. Momentarily, she felt alarmed because it was after dark and no one had ever come up on the ridge at night before. Immediately then, she realized that Rainbow's bark was one of welcoming recognition. She ran down the stairs, excitement making her heart thud. It had to be Clay. He'd come back from California. She breathed an explosive sigh of elation.

Rainbow stood in front of the door, his tail wagging like a rapid tempo metronome. "Hey boy. Get Racile to let me in." Clay hollered through the door, at the same time knocking briskly again.

"I'm right here," she hollered back. Turning the lock, she opened the door. "Golly, you surprised me. I expected you to stay in Hollywood for weeks maybe." She spoke quickly, blinking her eyes in order to see him standing in the shadowed darkness. "What are you doing back so soon?"

"Let me in and I'll tell you." He pushed her gently to one side and took a step forward, leaning one shoulder against the door frame.

She stared up at him. How tall he seemed! Perhaps it was because he was wearing a brown business suit and she had only seen him before in casual sports clothes.

"Should I stand on ceremony and wait for you to ask me in?" He leaned his head closer to her, looking at her in an appraising manner. "You're going to allow me to come in, aren't you?" Though he phrased it as a question, he stated it as a fact. Then brushing against her, he immediately stepped inside the entry hall. Bending down, he gave Rainbow a hearty rub on the head. "You're glad to see me, aren't you boy?" He straightened as Racile pushed the door shut behind him. "How did you and this dog of mine get along?" he inquired. "Hope he didn't make any trouble for you." Clay let his eyes travel over her as he spoke.

"He was no trouble at all. I was happy to have his company." She rolled down the sleeves of her yellow blouse, fumbling nervously with the buttons at the cuffs. The way he had been looking at her made her conscious that although her butter-colored slacks had been freshly laundered when she'd first put them on that morning, they were wrinkled now and even smudged with some dust from the books she'd handled upstairs. She brushed at the front of her slacks as she led the way into the living room. Sitting down at one end of the couch, she continued talking about the big collie. "It would have seemed pretty solitary here at night without Rainbow."

"Solitary?" Clay scoffed, taking off his coat and tossing it over the Windsor chair. "I thought from what Larry said that you were having a friend down from Philadelphia."

"I don't know what gave him that idea," she said, a small frown creasing her brow.

"He said you couldn't come to dinner with all of us because you were expecting a call from a friend in Philly. I guess I presumed your friend was coming up for a visit." He joined her on the couch.

Racile suppressed a smile, surprised by Clay's transparency. Obviously he was interested in finding out about any close friends she might invite to the Cape. "And I presume that because you're a playwright, you have to analyze everything—a

71

rejected dinner invitation, a telephone call from a friend—and make a little drama out of it," she countered lightly. "But if you're checking up on my social life in Briny Bay, I'll tell you. My nights were spent alone. My days were spent in the company of John Wharton. He repaired my roof while I did the painting."

"More rust-red doors and windows?" He cocked his head, narrowing one eye at her in a wink.

"Yes." Her eyes crinkled in a smile. "Now tell me about the screenplay. Are you going to write it here, or do you have to go back out to California?"

"Neither one," he said, moving closer to her on the sofa. "I'm not doing it."

"What do you mean? They're still going to make a movie of *Rainbow's End*, surely?"

"Yes, but I decided I didn't want to spend the time writing the adaptation. I discussed it with two screenwriters and gave them the suggestions I had. They'll do a first-rate job of it." He slid closer to her, laying his arm along the back of the couch. "All I could think about was getting back here to work on my new play. That's what's really important to me right now."

The image of Sylvia Sontag appeared like a genie in Racile's mind. How did she react to Clay's decision? she wondered. Not favorably, she could bet on that. "Was Sylvia upset when you left?" she asked in what she hoped would sound like an innocent question. "I know she was counting on your writing the screenplay so that it would be the right movie vehicle for her."

Clay's face seemed to tighten at the mention of Sylvia. He was sitting close enough too so that she felt his body tense. "Sylvia will shape the movie to her advantage without my help," he said sharply. "She's manipulated Larry, as she always does, and he's agreed to stay for several more days. By then, she'll have writers, musicians and the director moving heaven and earth to make her the shining star."

She looked at him trying to discover what emotions lay behind his words. Outside of the theater, what was the extent of Clay's relationship with Sylvia? Was it as personal as Larry's seemed to be? Was Clay jealous of Larry? Were they competing for the beautiful actress? She didn't like the questions that raced through her head. "Tell me about your new play," she said abruptly, wishing she'd never mentioned Sylvia and wanting to change the subject.

"It's more complex than anything Larry and I have tried before."

"What's it about?"

"People, relationships." He moved his hand from the back of the couch and brushed his fingers lightly across the nape of her neck. "And love," he added.

His nearness was having an unsettling effect on her and his touch made the back of her neck tingle. "But . . . what about the story . . . the actual plot of the play?"

"You ask as many questions as the backers." He laughed. "Do you want to put money in my play?"

"If I were rich, I might. But stop being evasive.

73

You make it sound as if this new work is more important to you than all your others. I want to understand why. I hate it when someone makes me this curious about something and then won't explain things to me," she said, a small frown forming on her brow. She still was far from understanding what could have caused Clay to leave Hollywood without writing the screen adaptation for *Rainbow's End.* It was inconsistent with what she'd seen of the importance he placed on his work. She knew he felt he could do a better job than any Hollywood screenwriter in adapting his own play for the movies. Why then would he consider letting someone else do the job for him? What was so important about this new play that it couldn't wait a few weeks, long enough for him to handle the screenplay. It was wholly illogical for him to have come back to Briny Bay so soon. She stared at him in undisguised appraisal, considering the emerging complexities of his actions and even his attitude when he came. Why was he here? She toyed with the buttons on the front of her blouse. For an instant she had the fleeting thought that it might have something to do with her.

"You can stop being curious," he said with a good-natured arch of his eyebrows. "The reason the new play is so important is because it has the potential of being big. It's not a light musical play like the others Larry and I have done. This is musical theater. We'd like to think this time we're creating something classic and lasting."

"Can you do that?"

"I have the material for it. All the ingredients are there. I need to study them, decide how best to use them, even if I can only use some of them." Abruptly his expression changed. His eyes were no longer light but shadowed and intent.

His statements puzzled her. "You talk about materials and ingredients as if you were mixing cement. That will make for a heavy drama," she joked.

Clay's arm slid off the back of the sofa and circled her shoulders. "Let's forget about my plays—past, and present and future—for awhile. I'd much rather discuss how I'm going to return a favor." He pressed her closer, settling her head into the hollow of his shoulder. He spoke now with a certain familiarity in his voice creating a mood of intimacy between them. She was aware that she was breathing rapidly due to feelings of excitement his closeness generated in her.

"What favor is that?"

"You fed and cared for Rainbow for a week. Now, I want to spend some time showing you Cape Cod." Clay's cheek rested against her hair and she felt the pleasant warmth of his breath brush her temple as he spoke.

"Do you really?"

"I wouldn't offer if I didn't. You already know that. Remember, you accused me before of not standing on ceremony." He laughed.

"Won't I interfere with your writing?" She lifted her head, moving so she could look at him. "I've already disturbed your privacy here on Hunter's Ridge. I don't want to keep you from the work you want to do on your new play." Her solemn expression deepened the color of her eyes to a soft purple.

"You're not going to interfere with my writing. In fact, you can inspire it." His expression became as serious as hers. "I might as well warn you that I intend to find out all that goes on in that lovely head of yours." He took her face between his hands, contemplating her. "I have an idea I may want to write a play about someone like you."

Was she imagining it or had he spoken a bit sharply? One thing she hadn't imagined was the firm, warm pressure of his palms cupping her chin. Clay's words and actions were confusing her, arousing feelings within her that she didn't know quite how to deal with. His words were flattering and he was regarding her with more than a casual interest. But something was not right. She didn't know what it was, but she did know it made her uncomfortable.

"In that case, there is one thing in particular I'd like to do," she said brightly, masking her uneasiness behind a forced smile. "I want to take the ferry to Martha's Vineyard."

"We'll do it then," he said, letting one hand drop down to rest against her neck and with the back of his fingers he stroked the soft skin beneath her chin. "I'll take you tomorrow. But we'll have to get an early start to reach Wood's Hole in time to catch the morning ferry."

The light touch of his fingers was causing Racile's pulse to accelerate. Without being conscious of doing it, she tilted her head back slightly as Clay caressed the hollow of her throat.

"I'll have to come over and get you out of bed before six o'clock. Better yet, I could just stay here tonight. Then I could make sure you got up in time." As he said this he gave her well-proportioned figure his full attention.

She flushed, realizing the white knitted shirt she was wearing hugged the soft contours of her breasts in a way that called attention to their fullness. "Don't worry. I'm an early riser," she said quickly. "Besides, I have a reliable alarm clock." She started to move away from him.

As if he'd anticipated her action, he slid his hand around the back of her neck, pulling her face to his. "Alarms go off with a jarring noise. I'd awaken you like this." Clay put his mouth to hers, touching her lips gently at first, then with a more insistent pressure. His lips were warm and as they searched hers any trace of resistance she might have had vanished. Her hands crept around his neck, while his warm hands moved to the center of her back, pressing her so close that she felt her round breasts crushed against the hardness of his chest. She responded to every pressure of his lips, of his body against hers and after a time she trailed her fingers sensually through the thick hair at the back of his neck.

He took his mouth from hers and gazed at her, his eyes darkly passionate. "Wouldn't you like that better than a noisy bell going off in your ear?" he asked, a smile pulling the corners of his mouth.

She took a deep breath. "I'd find the alarm safer." Sidling away from his arms, she got up from the couch. "It's getting late Clay, and if we're getting an early start tomorrow. . . ." Her voice trailed off. Clay was nodding his head at her.

"That's a cue to bring the curtain down on a scene, if I ever heard one." He laughed. "Not the way I'd write it however, but nevertheless the end of Act One." Clay slowly rose to his feet and Rainbow jumped up from the spot where he'd been sleeping and trotted over to join him.

Clay put his arm around Racile's waist and they walked together across the room. At the front door, he paused and stood for a minute looking down into her face. He kept his arm around her, holding her so close that Racile could feel his warm breath on her face. He didn't touch her cheek or move to kiss her again, but just looked at her with narrowed eyes.

"There's a myriad of things I want to know about you Racile."

"I doubt there's that much to learn." She laughed uneasily, wishing she weren't so absurdly conscious of the warm feeling caused by his arm circling her waist.

"Some *one* and some *thing* tells me there is." His voice took on the slightly brittle tone she thought she'd detected earlier.

She looked at him in growing apprehension. What did his cryptic words mean? At first she'd thought he meant his statements as a compliment. But was there an undercurrent of censure there as well? He was making her angry. Reaching for the door knob, she signified her wish to have him leave. "If you expect me to match wits with you Clay, it will have to wait until tomorrow." She opened the door as she spoke, ushering him out into the cool, black night. His face wore an inscrutable expression as he whispered a casual goodnight, then strode off with Rainbow at his heels.

A tight smile remained on Racile's lips until she had the door closed firmly after him. She stood there, her arms crossed over her chest, feeling a troubled anger creeping over her. What did Clay really mean by his words? Did he want to know all about her because he felt attracted to her? Certainly, she was highly aware of the attraction he held for her. Just the touch of his hand stirred her and the exciting impact of his kiss had affected her more than Burke's ever had. She had never felt so vulnerable to a man's caress before. She wanted to believe that Clay felt the same chemistry between them as she did. But if he did, why did he pretend that he saw her as some kind of a research project? Someone that he had to study? Hugging herself against the hurt of these thoughts, she pressed her fingers so firmly into the soft flesh of her upper arms, her fingernails made crescent marks on her skin. If Clay did see her that way, then he'd only come back from California in order to do his homework. She gave a wry laugh and without bothering to turn off the downstairs lights, she climbed the stairs to her bedroom.

Chapter Five

For some inexplicable reason, Racile had not returned the envelope of her mother's souvenirs to the shelf in Trenton Hunter's bedroom. Instead, she had placed it on the nightstand beside her own bed, propping it up against her travel alarm clock. Now as the persistent buzz of the alarm awakened her and she reached over to silence it, her hand closed over the top edge of the smooth paper. She sat up, sliding her shapely bare legs over the edge of the bed. She opened the flap of the envelope and shuffled through the slips of paper, pulling out the ferry ticket. For a moment, she stared at it, then with a smile, she tucked it back inside. All those years ago, a trip to Martha's Vineyard had been such a happy occasion for her mother that she'd kept the ferry ticket as a souvenir. Maybe it was romantic and foolish, but Racile wanted this day to be as special for her as it had been for Madelaine. Jumping off the bed, she headed for the shower. Her nerves were tingling, but she was determined not to let herself get uptight with Clay today. He'd said he wanted to know all about her. Well, she wanted to know everything about him too. This might well be a day of discovery for both of them.

She was ready and waiting at six-thirty when Clay came to pick her up. His eyes registered his approval as she walked out the door. "Whatever you call that outfit, I like it," he commented, letting his gaze comb her white divided skirt.

"They're culottes." She smiled, taking pleasure from his compliment.

They decided to drive her car to Wood's Hole because it would be more comfortable than Clay's jeep. As they walked around the corner of the house, Racile handed her car keys to Clay. "You drive 'cause you know the way. And while it's still so early in the morning, I want to see if I can't catch sight of some of your New England shore birds, a piping plover or a willet. I need a bird, I think, for one of my wallpaper designs for the house."

Clay had turned the car around and was now heading toward the gate to the main road. "By *the house*, I suppose you mean yours here on the ridge?" He scowled. "I'm still trying to get used to the red paint you put on the outside. Are you telling me that now you're going to force me to look at wallpaper all over the inside?"

"No," she retorted sharply. "The rooms I plan to paper are upstairs, mainly my bedroom. You'll never even see that."

He took one hand off the steering wheel and placed it firmly over hers. "I wouldn't bet on that if I were you," he said archly, giving her a roguish wink. They had reached the main road and Clay made the turn too fast, causing the car to fishtail in the loose gravel.

She moved his hand away, placing it on the steering wheel. "You can do a better job of driving my car if you use two hands," she teased, laughing. "And if you really want to see the wallpaper I'm designing for my bedroom, I'll make you a deal. You can see it when you help me hang it on the walls."

"That wasn't what I had in mind." His eyebrows flicked upward, and amusement danced in his umber eyes.

She turned her head and looked out the window to avoid continuing the conversation. Although he seemed to enjoy teasing her about the changes she was making—the red paint and the proposed wall paper—she wondered if he still felt some degree of resentment because she was here in his father's house. She hoped not.

The weather was fine. The wind felt fresh and fair, and Racile could see the high white clouds of early summer gather above the horizon, causing blue shadows to run across the sea. At the same time however the early morning light slanted along the shore and the brightening sun rays sparkled on the waves. One lone sailboat nudged the shore, its sail slatting in the soft wind.

"I think I'd like to learn to sail in a small boat like that one." She nodded in the direction of the knockabout.

"You would?" He sounded surprised.

"Sure. Is it terribly difficult?"

"Not when the wind and weather are right." His lips pressed together in a firm line. "Did you sail often with Trenton on his boat?"

"No, of course not. How could I?" Her searching glance noted the crease in Clay's forehead which now marred his smooth, suntanned features.

"That's right. I forgot that you told me you'd never been to the Cape before." He spoke sharply.

"You don't believe me, I know. But I can explain and I want to . . ."

"Don't bother," Clay interrupted. "Let's just say under the circumstances it does seem odd to me that Trenton wouldn't have brought you here to view the Cape and see the house he intended you to have."

"The circumstances, as you put it, are not what they seem. But since you don't want me to bother to explain, I won't." She clipped her words in anger, thinking that he was extremely opinionated and stubborn. "Let's just say that you make it impossible for you and me to discuss anything that has to do with your father and his house. Now let's drop the subject until you're in a more receptive mood. I don't want to spend the entire day arguing with you, Clay." With that, she lapsed into an icy silence. Meanwhile Clay appeared to center his attention on the highway.

At Wood's Hole they boarded the ferry. The boat was a double-decker with a white painted superstructure, ungainly, without grace of line. There was a large, enclosed cabin on the boat, but Clay led her to the upper deck. There were life preservers, as on an ocean liner, strung along the walls and directions for using them. The boat was not crowded, or at least few passengers had come topside, probably because the early morning fog had only just lifted, leaving a misty spray to wet the wind. Racile shook her head when Clay asked if she'd rather sit inside the cabin. She liked the feel of the fresh air on her face and welcomed the salty odor and the smell of seaweed. At that moment the ferry's deep-throated whistle emitted two hoarse and husky notes. There was a grinding sound, a sudden lurch, a rattle of chains, then movement.

"We're underway." Excitement danced in her eyes. "My first ferry ride."

Clay grinned as if he found her air of expectancy contagious. "We have a perfect day for it."

She leaned against the rail and looked out at the rolling, blue-green water, intrigued with the lacy caps of foam that topped each wave. Clay stood beside her and she knew he was watching her. She continued to gaze out over the water. Clay moved closer, leaning on the rail so that his arm and shoulder rested against hers.

"I'm glad you're not disappointed in this tub of a boat. It's slow going."

"Well, we're not in any hurry and the water is beautiful. It's a different color depending on where you look, blue, green, black . . . and across there where the sun touches it it's a silken silver gray." She indicated an area far off on the horizon. "I wish I could get a watered silk wall-covering in that exact color of gray." Clay looked where she was pointing, squinting his eyes against the sun. She noticed there was now a belligerent thrust to his chin. He thinks I'm talking about this color for more wallpaper for my house and he doesn't want to hear any more of my ideas on that subject, she thought. She leaned her head farther over the railing and stared down at the sides of the boat.

"When you called this ferry an old tub, did you mean that it really is old?" She asked pursing her lips thoughtfully. "I mean could it have been in use here fifteen years or so?"

"Easily. Probably twenty . . . thirty . . . even more. The Steamship Authority maintains it under strict regulations and frequent government inspections, however. Don't worry. It may be old, but it's sturdy and safe." He put his arm around her waist protectively. "And besides, you can count on me to toss you a life preserver if we start to sink." He hugged her, laughing and leaning over so his cheek touched the side of her hair.

"I'm not worried about sinking. I was just hoping this might be the same ferry my mother rode on to Martha's Vineyard a long time ago." She paused, shading her face with one hand, aware suddenly that the morning sun glaring off the water was stinging her eyes. "My mother spent part of one summer here at the Cape once. I know it sounds silly, but I think she'd have wanted me to see and do the same things she did here." Sighing softly, Racile blinked away the moisture that misted her eyes. "You see, it wasn't until after my mother died that I discovered that the few weeks she spent here were so important to her."

"And you want to make your time here important too." He spoke soberly and there was a gentle quality in his voice that she hadn't heard in it before. "Is that what you're saying?"

"Something like that."

"You might say I'm doing the same thing—making my time here important."

Racile turned her head and looked into his face. "How's that?"

"I know that Trenton left me my part of the ridge property because I'm a writer. It was his way to encourage me in my work."

"Clay, he was your father, for heaven's sake. He gave it to you because you're his son."

"No, it was because of my writing. If I hadn't become a playwright, I doubt if I would ever have had any contact with him at all." He spoke matter of factly, but his face reflected the deep emotions he felt for his father.

"How can you say that?"

"Because it's true. Trenton Hunter was never a father to me. I never even knew him until after the success of my first play. We met as writers then, never as father and son." He took his arm from around her waist and moving a step away from her, he turned his back to the water.

Racile turned around then too, and leaned back against the deck rail. "He never saw you, even once, while you were growing up?"

Clay shook his head.

"I can't believe he could possibly have been that detached, that unfeeling. Why, his books reveal that he was an emotional man, an emotional writer."

"You're right. He was both. That's why even when I couldn't understand him, I still wanted to be like him. Write with the intense passion and power that he did." There was both anger and admiration in Clay's voice. "And you don't think of him as an uncaring man, because he wasn't to you, of course." His glance swept over her. "You were the woman he loved. You were an important part of his life." There was no malice in his tone. She was glad for this.

Racile's eyes searched his face. She was wondering if there was any point in trying to explain now about her mother. Something warned her to be cautious. There was no reason to risk destroying the intimate mood between them. He was talking openly to her, giving her insights into his feelings. She mustn't let anything interrupt this.

"I know that my mother set down the rules for Trenton to follow where I was concerned. She was dead set on establishing a normal family life for me—mother, father, child, all bearing the same name. That's why she insisted Trenton allow my stepfather to legally adopt me. It probably was all for the best." He shrugged. "I can't honestly say it wasn't. It just accounts for the reason that Trenton Hunter was nothing more than a name to me until after I was grown. When my first play opened in New York, he arranged for us to meet." Clay wrapped his arms around his chest and his tension appeared to dissolve as he relaxed his shoulders. "I felt strange with him at first. He only talked about my play, so I talked about his novels." Clay looked over her head toward the ferry's bow, his hazel eyes filled with the memory. "Later he introduced me to his writer friends, two of whom had also gotten the Pulitzer. It meant a lot to me."

"Did his friends know you were his son?"

Clay's mouth compressed in a hard line. "He never mentioned it, if that's what you mean," he answered tersely.

Why had she asked? It was a thoughtless question. She wanted to sympathize, tell him she knew Trenton's attitude had hurt him deeply. Reaching out, she put her hand against the solid, tense muscles of his shoulder. "I'm sorry," she said lamely. It was all she could say.

"I'm not." His mouth eased. "Trenton encouraged my writing. We had that in common. It was enough. I know, too, that he expected me to branch out. Write something more meaty than musical comedy. Just a month before he drowned, he suggested that I adapt one of his novels for the stage."

Racile's eyes were suddenly luminous. "Oh, Clay," her voice rose an octave. "Then that's what you're doing. You're basing your new play on one of your father's novels. How marvelous!"

"Oh, you think so, do you?" He smiled at her elation, and since she still had her hand on his shoulder, it seemed natural for him to put his hands on either side of her waist and draw her closer.

"Which novel is it?"

"Not one that's been published. In fact, it's one he was only planning to write. He hadn't written any of it yet, when he died." He slid his arms around her, clasping his hands against her back as he spoke.

Aware of how close they were standing, she drew herself away from him so she could look into his eyes. "Are you teasing me?" she asked. "How can you take a book that isn't even written and make it into a play?"

"By using the material Trenton left, his detailed notes for the plot line, and the character descriptions which he'd completed. What I'm uncertain of is how he intended to resolve the conflicts of the story." Slanting his face closer to hers again, he tightened his arms around her. "Trenton's outline for the book was incomplete, just the beginning and the plot twists. I need to discover how he planned the ending."

"There's always . . . and so they lived happily ever after," she quipped in an attempt at levity. He seemed to be making a keen assessment of her reactions and she found this disquieting.

"Not always happy. Not always forever after either," he countered, his eyes clouding with passion, as he slowly brought his mouth down on hers. There was a throbbing in her veins that was like the steady, powerful beat of the boat's engines. She slipped her arms around his neck, yielding to him and returning his kiss. "I thought we were talking about the end to your play," she murmured, her fingers brushing the back of his hair.

"I'd rather talk about the beginning of us," he whispered with his lips still warm on hers. His hands, that had been at both sides of her waist, now moved slowly upward, sending a shudder of desire through her whole body as they touched her breasts.

"Someone will see us." She shivered and hid her face in the warm hollow of his neck, thrilled by the scent of him and the possessive feel of his hands caressing her.

"No they won't. We're alone up here. Everyone has gone below to their cars."

She lifted her head from his shoulder and her lips found his again. While they stood together, the song of the boat engines changed, dropping to a lower register. The boat was turning in an arc and moving into the dock. "We're there." She sighed and there was regret in her voice. She looked at Clay, wondering if he found the end of their journey as inopportune as she did.

He groaned huskily, stepping back, letting his hands slide reluctantly down her arms and catching her hands firmly in his. "We'd better go below and find the car." He led her toward the stairs to the lower deck.

She moved along beside him, not really conscious of what she was doing. She felt empty now, bereft of his arms and the feel of his mouth on hers. What was happening to her? She'd been stirred by a man before, but not like this, not at all like this. Was she an emotional fool, blown up like a balloon, floating in a fantasy, or had Clay truly meant it when he'd said that this was only the beginning for the two of them? Was that his reason for revealing his feelings about his father to her? They both had made some new discoveries about each other. And she wanted to believe she and Clay had begun to build a bridge of small intimacies across the seas of misconceptions that separated them. Racile entwined her fingers through Clay's and quickened her step.

Once they were on the island of Martha's Vineyard, they drove from Vineyard Haven to Edgartown, the oldest settlement on the island. It was a seafaring town of the early whaling days complete with charming old houses lining the narrow streets. They wandered around, taking in all of the sights. At a restaurant on the waterfront they ate chilled lobster remoulade and watched the small ships sailing around the point, a dream of motion on the blue plate of the harbor.

Following lunch, Clay took her to the wildlife sanctuary. "You can see every kind of bird you could possibly want to use for your wallpaper designs." He teased her, then explained about the two hundred some acres of beach, marsh and woodland area which harbored vast numbers of waterfowl. They followed the visitor trails and also toured the rehabilitation barn for crippled birds, where Racile made a quick sketch of a gray loon and a chocolate brown-backed sandpiper with greenish legs and a slender, straight bill.

The sun had moved slowly westward and a warm breeze blew from the south as they drove back along the streets of Edgartown, seeking out a historical house once owned by an illustrious captain of a whaling ship. Over the harbor the terns rose gracefully from the water's edge, flying out to join the gulls coasting out over the water.

"There's the place I want you to see," Clay pointed out a house on a slight rise overlooking the harbor. Racile thought the gray house looked a bit awesome and imposing with its railed widow's walk and long veranda framed with rambler roses. "It is after four," Clay said, glancing at his watch. "But if we hurry, I think I can persuade the attendant to allow us to view the inside of the house."

Bayberry and beach plum bushes lined the path to the front door lending a subtle fragrance to the warm afternoon air. Inside the house, however, the rooms were cool as the wind from the sea soughed through the screens with a soft murmuring sound. Racile gazed in fascination at the antique collections that filled several cabinets and cases in the parlor and central rooms of the house. There were snuffboxes and pillboxes made of fine metals and decorated with jade and coral. There were also delicate boxes made of tortoise, ebony and teak. Racile could not resist running her hand over the top of a small chest made of a strange dark wood inlaid with mother-of-pearl. Clay, on the other hand was fascinated by a brass compass and a scrimshaw whaling scene carved on a whale's tooth.

As they started upstairs, Racile stopped to examine a tall cabinet in the hall which held a display of seashells. "Look Clay, these shells are the same shape as a child's spinning top or a

Hindu's turban. Can't you just see them on pink and silver paper for an elegant bathroom?"

"No, I can't," he growled. "And furthermore, I don't want to. You could drive a man crazy with this fetish of yours to put everything you see on the walls." He laughed then and held out his hand to her, palm up. "Now you just come with me. I want to show you something."

"I told you I don't like bossy playwrights." She made a face at him, but at the same time without a moment's hesitation, she put her hand in his. Clay's fingers tightened around hers and he pulled her after him up the worn wooden stairs of the Victorian house.

When they reached the top level, he led her out on the narrow widow's walk where they stood close together looking out toward the blue vistas of the sea. Far out in the harbor the bell buoy struck. The clanging sound had a plaintive ring. "What a melancholy sound that is." Racile shivered, hunching her shoulders and running her hands along her upper arms. The wind coming off the water felt cold to her. "Just standing out here makes me feel lonely. I certainly was not cut out to be the wife of a sea captain."

"Oh, I don't know." Clay regarded her with a thoughtful expression. "Those old sea captains carried rich cargos and most of them became wealthy men. You'd have been provided with a fine house by the sea. It would have been filled with fine things gathered from all over the world just for you. Isn't that exactly what you would have wanted?"

Racile lifted her head sharply, staring at his composed but stern features. Was he making a joke? Or was he making an oblique reference to M.R. Douglas and Trenton Hunter. "Are you asking a question or making a judgment?" she demanded, pressing her hand to her brow as she watched him with troubled, angry eyes.

"I'm sorry, but I have to ask you two to come in now." The custodian of the historical house spoke to them from the open doorway. "You see, we're closing for the day."

The interruption prevented Clay from responding. Frowning heavily, he put his hand under her elbow. "We have to leave. We can talk about this in the car."

"No, let's forget it." She jerked her arm from his grasp and proceeded quickly from the balcony. There was nothing to be gained by discussing his resentful attitude. She knew, of course, that he was passing judgment on her again. On her mother actually, but he had no way of knowing that. Well, though she'd been tempted to explain everything to him before, she was now beginning to feel hesitant. If she told him the truth, he'd only condemn Madelaine. She could just imagine how Clay would feel about a married woman with a nine-year-old child, who as a result of a brief summer affair acquired the house and treasured possessions of his father. Pressing her lips together until they were white, Racile walked as rapidly as she could down the two flights of stairs and out of the house. She felt suddenly as if she might cry.

As they drove to the ferry terminal, they were

careful to talk only about superficial things. There had been few passengers coming over, but there were many more for the return. Racile climbed to the upper deck with Clay, but by mutual consent they chose seats toward the front on the port side instead of walking the deck or standing by the rail. When the cool, early evening winds began to blow, he slipped his arm around her shoulders. Even though she accepted his gesture as meaningless, she remained within the curve of his arm, resting her head against the solid muscles of his shoulder. For some time neither of them said anything. If the people around them were talking, Racile took no notice. She closed her eyes and wished that she and Clay were alone on a mythical barge that was carrying them into the immensity of the sea. After a time she felt Clay turn his head and lower his face so he could kiss her forehead. Perhaps it was foolish, but when she felt the warmth of his lips against her temple, she experienced a sense of physical release, as if all the accumulated tension in her body was escaping. Her nerves were tingling but they were no longer tense.

On the drive back to Briny Bay they stopped at the largest supermarket along Route 6 and made a fast tour of the grocery aisles to select what they needed for dinner.

Later they ate by candlelight in Racile's house; the soft flickering points of light at each end of the oval cherry table cast haloes around their faces as they dined on the steaks they'd prepared together. Then, feeling mellowed by the intimate meal, they settled down on the couch in the living room. Clay had a brandy and Racile sipped Curacao from a delicate crystal, liqueur glass.

"I want to ask you about the Cape Cod series of designs you're doing. What are you putting in them besides seashells and sandpipers?"

She shot him a curious glance over the rim of her glass. Her wallcovering designs were the last subject she'd expected him to bring up. "I thought you said this afternoon that you were tired of hearing about this *fetish* of mine?" She tossed his earlier words back at him.

Cupping his brandy glass between his hands, he rotated it slightly, swirling the dark amber liquid in the bottom of the glass. "A good playwright must recognize when the dialogue needs rewriting. I realize a couple of my lines didn't read well today." She detected nothing facetious in Clay's tone. Could he mean this as an apology of sorts?

"To answer your question, add sand, surf and sailboats to the shells and shore birds." She slurred her s's impishly, feeling a degree of satisfaction in the thought that he was expending his charm to make amends.

"What, no lighthouse?"

"No lighthouse." She laughed.

"I hope you'll let me have a look at them before you send them to your company in Philadelphia." He leaned over to set his brandy glass on the sea chest in front of the sofa. "I'm particularly interested in the design you've done for your bedroom. I really want to examine it both before and after it goes on your walls." As he spoke he deliberately removed Racile's glass from her hand

and set it down beside his. Taking her into his arms, he brushed his lips across her cheek. "Especially *after*," he dropped his voice to a whisper, trailing kisses along her ear.

Racile's pulse accelerated with his light caress. "I could go get some of my designs and show them to you now," she whispered back, laying her hand flat against his chest as if she might try to push him away. Instead, however, she spread her fingers so that she could touch the warm skin exposed by his open-necked shirt.

"You're not moving from this couch to show me anything." He gave a low chuckle and eased her down against the soft cushions. "Every beautiful thing I want to look at is here beside me." Her bronze hair glowed in the soft lamplight. Clay smoothed the silken strands back from her face before he kissed her forehead, the corners of her eyes and the tip of her nose. "You are very beautiful Racile." He traced her face with his fingers and she found the sensuous touch of his hands as exciting as his lips had been. "No wonder your heart-shaped face and those intriguing violet eyes inspired a novel." She was so conscious of his fingers moving over her throat and neck that she didn't hear all of his words.

He was looking at her profoundly, his eyes darkening as he moved his hand along the front of her blouse, then slipped it beneath the fabric.

"Wh . . . what did you say about a novel?" she murmured, closing her eyes. Her skin was tingling under his touch that moved erotically across her skin, tantalizingly close to her breasts.

"Racile, I don't want to talk anymore," Clay

said, his eyes now mirroring his passion. His mouth met hers, opening her lips to kiss her deeply.

She brought her hands up to his neck, unable to keep from touching him. Clay slid his arms around her, pressing her to him. As his kiss deepened his searching mouth moved on hers with a more insistent demand. Racile responded to the pressure of his lips, of his body against hers. Within her, desire flowed warm and heavy in a response that was new to her, more exciting and disturbing than she'd ever known before. Her heart was beating in a chaotic rhythm. She fingers glided sensually along the back of his neck and as the passion mounted between them, his uneven breathing was proof that she had aroused him as much as he had aroused her.

Clay moved his lips from hers, looking at her through smoldering, heavy-lidded eyes. "Let me make love to you, Racile."

Their eyes met, his asking, hers shadowed with uncertainty. He shaped her body with his hands. She sighed, filled with an indisputable awareness of her feelings for him. She was in love with him, deeply and completely. She reached up and touched the tiny lines that radiated from the corners of his hazel eyes, then trailed her trembling fingers over the arch of his strong cheekbones and down to lightly press against his wide mouth.

He kissed her fingertips and tightened his arms around her again. Reason told her to pull away at this moment or else there would be no turning back. Her body, however, had a will of its own.

She arched against him and her parted lips met his once more in a triumph of desire over caution.

For several lovely, timeless moments their lips spoke against each other, murmuring, laughing and making small wordless sounds. Then still holding Racile in the cocoon of his arms, Clay gently drew her from the couch. Easing his embrace so she could walk beside him, he led her toward the stairs.

Outside, the quiet of the night was suddenly broken as Rainbow began to bark and growl. Racile shot a questioning look toward Clay and then let out a startled gasp as a loud knock sounded at the front door.

"Whoever that is, he's got rotten timing!" Clay's brow knotted in frustration. He held his hand out to indicate that she was to stay where she was. Then turning on his heels, he strode angrily to the door.

Chapter Six

Rainbow continued barking. Snapping on the outside light, Clay cracked open the front door. "What is it?" he asked, his irritation obvious.

"Sorry to bother you, but I'm looking for Racile Douglas. Is this her place?"

"Burke!" Racile cried out in surprise, hearing his familiar voice. "For heaven's sake." She ran to the door.

Clay opened the door wide and stepped back so the man could enter. The muscles of Clay's body seemed to tighten, and Racile felt his eyes on her face, as he noted her every reaction to Burke's arrival.

"I can't believe it. What are you doing here? Why didn't you let me know you were coming?" With a rush of words she tried to camouflage the awkwardness of the situation.

"I wanted to see you, darling." He grabbed her in a bear hug. "I was lonely these past weeks without you. I missed you."

She could feel her face flush. Clay took in every detail of the affectionate reunion scene. Pulling away from Burke, she turned to Clay, her eyes begging for his tolerance in this situation which was difficult as well as embarrassing for her. "Clay, this is Burke Mitchell, a friend of mine from Philadelphia."

"I gathered as much," he said with a wry smile. "Clay Forrest." He extended his hand to Burke. "I'm Racile's friend in Briny Bay." He continued to smile and his tone was deceptively placid.

"Clay's my neighbor. He . . . he owns the other house here on the ridge. The one you passed." She pointed in the direction of Clay's house. Both her voice and her pointing finger shook, revealing her nervousness. Quickly, she balled her hands and pressed them against the sides of her body. Struck suddenly by a bizarre thought, she lifted one hand to the front of her blouse, feeling the buttons and then as surreptitiously as she could, she rebuttoned the top three up to her throat.

This action did not go unnoticed by Clay. He arched his brows in amusement, his eyes flashing an intimate message to her which caused her face to flame. "Yes, Racile and I are actually joint tenants here. We share everything," he paused, "the entire ridge, the gate and the road." He paused again, as if he wanted to make what he was saying convey a special significance. "Even the affection and companionship of a collie dog.

Over these past two weeks I'd say the two of us have worked out a good neighbor policy that's mutually agreeable. Haven't we, Racile?"

Refusing to meet his mocking gaze, she turned her head, her lips set in a forced smile.

Burke's blue eyes now flashed with a competitive glint. "Mighty good of you to look out for my girl here," he retaliated, possessively putting his arm around Racile's shoulders.

The muscle twitched along Clay's jaw. "Well, I'll be getting back to my place," he said, looking directly into Racile's troubled eyes. "I'll remember where it was we left off and I want you to do the same."

A light of desire sparked for an instant in the dark glance that seared Racile's face. She felt what was left of her composure splinter and she thought she would choke on her sharply drawn breath. If Burke sensed the intensity of the drama between her and Clay, he did not let on. He did, however, tighten his hold around her shoulders.

Without another word to Racile, Clay gave a curt nod at Burke and walked out the open door. As he stepped off the front step, he thrust both hands deep in his pockets and strode off toward his own house. As Racile pushed the front door shut she heard Rainbow greet his master with a low, affectionate growl. Fixing a bright smile on her lips, she took Burke's arm. "Come on now and let me show you my nice old saltbox house. Then I want to hear about your plans for your new job in Albany." She didn't want to give Burke a chance to ask her questions about Clay or what he had been doing here in her house with her. "Did you have any trouble finding my house? Really Burke, you should have let me know you were coming." She kept on talking as she led him away from the door and into the living room.

Before nine the next morning, Racile was outside with her can of rust-red paint. She had only three more windows left to cover and this seemed the time to do it. The tensions of the previous night remained. She felt like a tightly coiled spring, wound to the limit; one more turn and she would snap. Filling the brush with the red-brown paint, she concentrated her energies on the window frame. Surely her rhythmic strokes would serve as therapy of sorts. She hoped to forget her troubled emotions by submerging them in this mundane activity.

When she first came outdoors, she caught sight of Clay walking along the edge of the ridge with Rainbow. He must have seen her as well, for she noticed now that he was heading back and had broken into a running gait. He had his white duck pants rolled up above his ankles, and his blue shirt was unbuttoned and sailed out behind him as he ran.

"Well, well, I'd have thought you had something more exciting to do this morning than paint windows. Where's your friend, Mitchell?" He came up next to her and began to button his shirt over his suntanned chest.

"He left ages ago. He had to be in Albany by ten-thirty this morning."

"Why is that?"

"I didn't think you'd be interested, but Burke quit his job in Philadelphia to join an accounting firm in Albany."

"My, my." Clay moved to stand close to her, looking over her shoulder, watching her paint. "In that case he went miles out of his way for such a brief visit with you. Hardly seems worthwhile." He put his hands on her shoulders and leaned his face next to hers. "Or was it?" The harshness of his voice grated in her ears as unpleasantly as the stubble on his chin scratched the tender skin of her cheek.

She pulled her head away to escape the contact. "You haven't shaved," she complained.

"And you haven't answered my question."

"I don't intend to." She turned to face him, her chin jutting out in anger. "Your question is crude and your manner is insulting. I don't like either." She continued her painting, whipping the brush back and forth across the wood sill with a vengeance.

"All right. Maybe I was out of line." He modified his tone. "But I'm sure you realize that this Burke's arrival was not the ending I wanted to our evening together. And furthermore, I found his proprietary way with you as offensive as hell."

Her eyes flared. Was Clay jealous? He sounded that way. The thought sent tremors of excitement racing through her. She leaned over and laid the brush on top of the paint can, keeping her head bent so he couldn't see the emotions mirrored on her face.

As she bent over her close-fitting tee-shirt

pulled free of the waistband of her jeans. Clay's strong hands suddenly circled her bare midriff. He helped her straighten and then turned her toward him.

"Under the circumstances I think you owe me more of an explanation. Briny Bay is hardly on the interstate between Philadelphia and Albany. I don't buy the story that your friend was passing through the area and suddenly just dropped by for a casual visit."

She was finding it difficult to act indifferent to the exciting warmth of Clay's hands as his fingers gently kneaded the tender area of her rib cage. "He came to find out if I'd decided to move to Albany with him. Burke's asked me to marry him."

"Marry him!" Taken back by Racile's announcement, his hands fell from her waist. "No wonder he acted possessive! You two must know each other quite well if he's expecting you to go to Albany with him as his wife." Clay was now tense; his shoulders were rigid, his jaw locked. Only his eyes moved in a raking scrutiny of her face. "I'm curious, Racile. Tell me, how long-standing is this *friendship* with this accountant of yours?"

Her hand crept to her throat and her eyes searched his uncertainly. "I . . . I've known him over a year. We've gone out together regularly. If that's what you're asking."

"You don't believe in lengthy mourning periods then?" There was a harsh edge to his voice.

"Mourning period? What are you talking

about?" She caught the corner of her lip between her teeth. Apprehension swept over her like a prairie fire.

"I'm talking about my father, about Trenton Hunter." Clay grabbed her, his fingers angrily cutting into the soft flesh of her upper arms. "Your grief over his drowning was so slight, so brief as to be nonexistent. You wasted no time after the loss of one love before you took on another. And even with your obvious charms, it had to take you some time to inflame this Burke Mitchell to the point of a marriage proposal." His gold-flecked eyes moved slowly over her body with an insulting thoroughness. "You know what I think? I think you were already involved with Mitchell at the same time that you were using your trickery and deceit to inveigle Trenton out of his house and his possessions."

A fury of emotions raged inside her. "You know a lot of ugly words Clay, but none of them have anything to do with why I'm the one who now has the deed to your father's house." She fought for control as tears of anger and frustration blurred her eyes. "There's so much you don't understand. . . ."

"Spare me the injured innocent act," he interrupted her, his voice caustic. "I'm not a fool. I've been around all kinds of self-seeking women. Heaven knows the theater is full of them. I've seen the lengths to which they'll go to get what they want for themselves, money . . . fame . . . property."

Tremors shook her body. She braced her legs and clenched her hands, but tightening her muscles only made the shaking worse. "And do you believe your father left this house to that kind of woman?"

The lines around Clay's mouth contracted as if he were in physical pain. Dropping his hands from her arms, he stepped away from her.

Racile had never seen him so tense, the muscles of his face and neck were taut, his movements jerky. His piercing look penetrated her eyes as if to read her thoughts, decipher her motives. As his eyes held hers, something that she couldn't understand seemed to stretch there between them, a feeling that knew no words, quivering in the silence.

"I don't know what to believe." Turning abruptly, he thrust both hands into his pockets and strode across the road to his jeep. Rainbow scamped along at his side.

Racile's hand was at her throat as she stood still, staring after him. She opened her mouth to call to him, to ask him to come back and listen to her while she explained about the deed. No sound came from her throat. Frozen with shock, she watched Clay climb in his jeep, snap his fingers at Rainbow and order the collie to jump in beside him. A second later, there was the sound of the motor whirring and as the Jeep moved forward with rapidly increasing speed, the tires sprayed a fan of sand. She could no longer see clearly. It was not, however, the cloud of sand in the air that obscured her vision, but her own helpless tears.

Racile went back to her painting without enthusiasm. She could no longer find pleasure in the task. It was merely something she had started and needed to finish. The day wore on and Clay did not return to the ridge. From time to time through the late afternoon and evening, Racile checked to see if the jeep was parked beside Clay's house. It was not. If he planned to return at all, which she doubted, it was going to be late in the evening. There were no lights in his house when she went to bed at eleven.

The following morning, Racile was up before seven. As soon as she was dressed, she walked over to Clay's. He was not there and neither was Rainbow. Obviously he wanted to avoid her and he was going to a good deal of trouble to do so. If he had left Briny Bay, he had taken Rainbow with him. This was not his usual pattern. She knew his habit was to have John Wharton come over once a day to feed the collie whenever he had to go into New York to see about one of his plays. Why was he reacting to their argument like this? Did Clay actually believe she intended to marry Burke? Could it matter to him? She pressed trembling fingers against her temples. Her head felt like a tightly wound up toy, madly running around in circles, making her dazed and confused. Slowly she went back to her own house.

By the time she had finished breakfast, she had made a decision about what she was going to do. She packed a bag and gathered up all the wallpaper designs she had made, putting them in the back seat of her car. Remembering Clay's warning about the rainstorms, she made a careful check of the windows before locking the front door and leaving.

At the Wharton's, she stopped to leave the keys. "I have to take care of some work in Philadelphia," she explained to the caretaker's wife. "I'll be gone a couple of weeks, maybe more. If you or Mr. Wharton see Mr. Forrest, you might tell him where I've gone. I didn't talk to him before I left. I guess he may be away too." She was deliberately fishing for information about Clay, wondering if Mrs. Wharton knew where he was, and knowing if he had left Briny Bay he would have had to leave his house keys with her.

Her gray head moved in a brief nod. "I'll tell him," was her only reply.

Back in Philadelphia, Racile made an effort to keep busy with her work. She was excited about her designs for the New England series of wall-coverings and anxious to see them in production. The pattern with the shore birds which she wanted for her bedroom would need a solid color coordinate to harmonize with it. Racile's own preference was for a delicate and soft tint of blue. She ordered the production of two grasscloths as well, knowing these would appeal to buyers. The design she had created using the sea shells from the house at Martha's Vineyard was to be executed in three color combinations: blush pink and silver, pale yellow and amber and coral red with pearl grey. She ordered these to be done in washable vinyls for use in bathrooms. Recalling the day Clay had accused her of wanting to cover every wall in her saltbox house with patterned wallpaper, she pursed her lips in a thoughtful expression. Though she had assured him that she only planned on using one of her designs and that only on the walls of her bedroom, now seeing the others being made ready for manufacture, she knew she had to put the seashells in the pink and silver in the small bathroom downstairs. Speculating about his reaction to the shell design, she frowned. At this point it would appear Clay had no interest in anything that she did. He certainly had not tried to reach her since she had left Briny Bay.

Although she spent a lot of time at the company, she tried to be at the carriage house most evenings and every morning. In fact, she had made a practice of staying at home as late as she dared each morning and still allow time to make it into the office before ten. In the back of her mind was always the hope that Clay would telephone. After all he knew the number. He had called her that first morning, so many weeks ago, just at the time she had been ready to leave for work. Why didn't he call her now? If he cared about why she had left or if he wanted her to come back, wouldn't he have called? She'd been in Philadelphia for ten days. John Wharton must have let him know that she had gone. She tortured herself with unanswered questions and negative thoughts.

Every day she grew more restless. She began to make arrangements so she could get back to the Cape. The Wallcovering Information Bureau had come out with their predictions of what was gaining in public popularity. It appeared that romantic florals, as well as Oriental and French designs which create a soft opulent look in a room, were preferred for the next year's line.

Armed with this information, Racile headed back to Briny Bay, promising to mail in some new designs within the next eight weeks.

The return trip seemed endless. And perhaps because she was so eager to be back, the heavier weekend traffic and the delays made her nervous and irritable. If she had used her head instead of her heart, she would have waited until Monday to drive to the Cape.

It was late afternoon when she caught sight of the blue ribbon of Cape Cod sky and sea fringed with low rays of golden sun. Relaxing her foot on the accelerator, she lowered the car window so she could hear the sounds of the sea sliding silkily upon the oyster white sands. She continued driving at this leisurely rate until after she left the Wharton's and headed toward Hunter's Ridge. Topping a slight rise in the road, she saw a gray compact car speeding toward her. In seconds the distance vanished between them. The driver of the compact began to honk repeatedly at the same time waving a slender hand out the window, flagging her down. Racile was close enough now to determine that those vividly lacquered nails, fluttering in the air like a cardinal's wing, belonged to Sylvia Sontag.

"What a darn shame. You're coming back just as I have to leave." Sylvia hollered to Racile as their two cars drew alongside each other and they both stopped. "You'll never know how desperately I needed you this weekend, Racile. I longed for someone nice to talk to. Clay was in a foul humor, and Larry was only a slight degree more cooperative. I could have cheerfully murdered them both

111

and I would have too, if I hadn't needed them both alive to write another song for me." She arched her brows dramatically. "After all, I am the star of *Rainbow's End*. Therefore I need more songs than my co-star. Couldn't you have thought Clay would see that? But no, he's in such a frenzy over this new play of his. You can't possibly imagine how vile he was because of my surprise visit. He says that I interrupted them." As if exhausted by the torrent of words, she blew a deep sigh of exasperation through her artfully shaped lips, hunching her shoulders drawing them close around her neck dramatically.

"Them . . . ? Then you do mean that Larry was here with you too?"

"Larry's been up there with Clay for ten days or more. The two of them have evidently been working like fiends on the latest play. Why, they're both submerged in it to the point of drowning! Honestly Racile, I had to call them from Hollywood three times, telling them I need-ed another song for the movie." She raced on with another outpouring of heated words. "Clay ignored me. If I hadn't flown here and threatened to stay until they wrote me a song, I'd never have gotten them to do it." She glanced quickly at the jeweled watch on her wrist. "Oh, I wish I didn't have to dash, but I must. I have to get this rental car to the Boston airport and get my flight back to California." Curling her fingers around the steering wheel, she rapidly drove off.

Racile's mind clutched at the crux of Sylvia's statements. Larry had been at Briny Bay with Clay for ten days or more. Most of the time she had been in Philadelphia, Clay and Larry had been together working on their new production. That meant Clay had been caught up in his writing and therefore he couldn't have had time to dwell about being angry or upset with her. He probably had forgotten the argument they'd had the morning following Burke's arrival at her house. She wanted to believe that this might be the case. If it were, perhaps there was a chance the two of them could pick up where they had left off before Burke came. Remembering the exciting moments which preceded that interruption, she felt her heart hammer in her breast and a flush of warm desire spread through her. Quite suddenly she was all aglow, feeling alive and full of love. She thought of that moment on the boat when Clay had said he wanted it to be a beginning between them. They had gone beyond mere beginnings now. Surely Clay knew that too. With this thought, she drove toward the rays of the setting sun. The sun looked like a fiery opal resting on the crest of the ridge causing a myriad of tiny colors to dance in front of her eyes, in much the same way that the sparks of hope danced through her mind.

Turning in at the gate, she took a deep breath and let it out slowly. She realized her heart had not resumed its normal pattern; she still felt a heavy pulsating in her chest, throbbing against her eardrums. Driving slowly, she kept the car in the grooved ruts of the road. As she drew near Clay's house, Rainbow trotted out to meet her and chased after her car, waiting until she had parked beside her own house before welcoming her with two friendly barks. Opening the car door and climbing out, she gave Rainbow a pat on the white diamond of hair that marked the top of his head. The collie wagged his plumelike tail. Racile smiled. At least Rainbow was glad to have her back on the ridge. She took that for a good omen.

Chapter Seven

The phone was ringing as Racile entered the house. Setting her suitcase down at the foot of the stairs, she ran into the kitchen to answer it.

"I'm glad you're back." The warmth in Clay's voice caused her heart to lurch. How happy those four simple words made her feel at this moment! "Larry and I are taking you out to dinner tonight. In fact, he claims he already has a date with you. That you promised weeks ago to have dinner with him the next time he came to Briny Bay."

"He's right, I did," she answered gaily, letting her pleasure at his invitation show in her voice. Though it was inanely foolish, she was smiling into the phone and oddly, the hand which gripped the receiver felt alive and warm. It was as if Clay's hand was pressed to hers.

"Good. He and I have only a little more work to do before we stop for the day. What say we come and get you in half an hour?"

"No, Clay!" She gasped in mock dismay. "You have to give me more time than that. I just walked in the door after driving all day. I've got to have time to make myself pretty if I'm having supper with two handsome men." Her words were punctuated by breathless laughter. "You keep working and let me shower and change. I'll just walk on over when I'm ready."

"Okay, but don't take too long. I want to see you."

On the surface it was an ordinary, prosaic statement, but she was aware of an undercurrent that left her with a feverish sensation. He was glad she was back and he wanted to see her. It was what she needed to hear him say.

Hope was warm inside her as she moved quickly through the house, opening windows to allow a fresh air to flow through the rooms. Outside the day was drawing toward a close and the setting sun cast soft, golden shadows across the top of the ridge.

As she climbed the stairs, she wondered what she should wear to dinner. It had been now two weeks and two days since she had seen Clay. She wanted to look as pretty as she could for this reunion. In her bedroom, she quickly shed her clothes and hurried into the bathroom.

After she had showered, she smoothed scented lotion over her body, and finished by adding touches of her most expensive perfume to her earlobes and the insides of her wrists. Wrinkling her nose like a contented rabbit, she recalled that she had bought this subtle but provocative fragrance both for its intriguing floral scent and its romantic French name, which translated to "Night of Love." She shrugged her bare shoulders and laughed at herself. At times she was excessively sentimental.

Knowing that Clay and Larry had been viewing the glamorous Sylvia this weekend prompted her to want to dress with flair and a show of sophistication. She put on a citron-colored linen dress. Its simple design was perfectly executed to complement the lovely proportions of her slender body. Looping an ivory chiffon scarf becomingly around her neck she decided against earrings; she would wear only her mother's emerald ring.

There was a lopsided, early-rising moon in the blue sky. Racile could just see its pale outline as she walked toward Clay's house. Because it was a warm night, Clay had the windows open and his front door stood ajar. As she stepped up on the porch, she heard the voices of the two men. They seemed to be shouting angrily at each other.

"You've never for a moment considered her feelings. How long are you going to deceive her, Clay?"

"Knock it off, Larry. I want you to keep the hell out of this. Do you understand that?" Clay's voice was harsh and commanding.

"You have to tell her what you're planning to do. For God's sake, man, level with her right now."

Racile was so caught up in what she was hearing, that she was unconscious of the fact that she was actually eavesdropping. She guessed that they were talking about Sylvia. Larry must be referring to Clay's apparent decision not to allow Sylvia to star in the new production. She was stunned when she heard Clay's next words.

"I'll tell Racile what I like, when I like," he said loudly. "I'm writing this script. It may have your music but it's my play, you know!"

"More like your obsession," Larry snarled. "You're completely irrational about every aspect of it."

"What the hell do you mean by that?"

"You see this work as a way to form a bond between you and your father. That's all that seems to be important to you. It's time you gave some thought to whether you may hurt someone else while you're accomplishing this."

There was a sudden silence as if Clay were taking time to consider what Larry had said. After a few moments he spoke again in a quieter voice. "If my father had lived to write this himself, I know it would have been his finest novel. My intention is to make absolutely certain that the play is the story Trenton Hunter intended to write. That's what's important to me. Call it a bond between us, if you like. I see it as the only way I have to add to the memory of the man who gave me life." He spoke slowly and his words were heavy with emotion.

Racile swallowed her breath in a painful gasp. She couldn't bear to hear another thing. It had been wrong of her to stand outside on Clay's porch and listen to even one word of the argument between Clay and Larry. "Come out, you two," she called through the screen door. "I'm here now and ready to go to dinner." Her voice shook and she sounded as tense and uncomfortable as she felt. Needing to camouflage her embarrassment, she made a show of rapping her high heels in an impatient staccato on the steps of the front porch. "Hurry along, because I'm starving. I'll wait for you in the jeep." Flinging the words over her shoulder, she ran down the steps and around the corner of the house to where the car was parked.

Five minutes later, she heard the screen door bang and then Clay strode up to the side of the jeep where she sat waiting. "Larry is coming out in a few minutes to take you to dinner," he said belligerently. "I'm afraid I can't go with you as I planned. I'm sorry."

He didn't sound sorry, but rather defiant and hostile. Racile glanced at him questioningly. "You . . . you're not coming with us? But why not?" As soon as she'd asked, she wished that she had not, for Clay's glowering expression intensified in response to her words.

"I have work to finish for one thing. Sylvia was here this weekend and interrupted everything I had planned to accomplish. On top of that, Larry just informed me he's leaving first thing in the morning." Anger and irritation underlined his every word.

She tried to think of something to say, but didn't want to reveal that she had overheard part of the argument he'd had with Larry. Before any comment came to mind, Larry appeared, and without a word to Clay, he took the driver's seat and jabbed the key into the ignition. Still ignoring Clay, he leaned his head toward Racile. "I've been looking forward to having dinner with you since you promised weeks ago." His eyes appraised her warmly. "I made reservations at an interesting place I think you'll like in Falmouth. So let's be on our way." He turned the key and the engine caught noisily.

Racile raised her hand in a quick wave toward Clay. She frowned as they drove off down the road to the gate. Being caught in the middle of such fierce animosity between the two men had given her a very uncomfortable feeling. She was filled with curiosity, but at the same time strangely apprehensive. She had the feeling that if she understood all that Clay and Larry were arguing about, it would only make her unhappy. She leaned back in her seat, determined to stop thinking about Clay for the remainder of the evening.

There weren't many people in the restaurant at Falmouth harbor at this hour on a Sunday night. The candles on the small, round tables for two created an intimate, romantic atmosphere. Larry ordered a chilled bottle of Chablis and as she drank the wine, Racile began to relax and enjoy the pleasant surroundings and Larry's entertaining conversation. The candles threw shadows on his face and his dark eyes gleamed as he told her stories of the early productions of his and Clay's musical comedies.

The waiter removed their salad plates and served the Beef Wellington as Larry was regaling her with his first traumatic encounter with Sylvia

Sontag: transposing an entire musical score to fit the range of her voice. Quite obviously, he felt the actress's real assets were her beauty and acting ability—not her singing talent.

Since he had brought up Sylvia's name, Racile told him of her encounter with the woman on the road that afternoon. "Sylvia said her visit this weekend put Clay in a foul mood."

Larry shrugged. "It wasn't a comfortable weekend for any of us. It started badly and just got steadily worse."

"With you and Clay working so hard on the new play, I can see how Clay would resent her interrupting and asking for a new song to be written immediately."

Spreading butter on a hot roll, he ate a bite of it before making a comment. "Hell or high water can't deter Sylvia when she wants something. She proved to be a total distraction every minute she was here."

"I gathered from seeing her with Clay before that she was rather a special distraction for him. Isn't that the case?" She raised her eyebrows questioningly.

Larry returned her look of speculation. "Well now," he said with a wry smile. "Are you asking me if Clay has more than a professional interest in his leading lady? If so, the answer is no. Sylvia is an asset to him on stage in our musical productions, but Clay's interest in her begins and ends right there."

"Does your interest end there too?"

"You don't believe in beating around the bush, do you?"

She flushed. "I'm sorry," she said lifting her napkin to her mouth. "I didn't mean . . ."

"Yes you did, Racile," he said with a laugh. "And I'd be flattered at your interest, except I somehow get the very distinct impression that you're more concerned with the depth of Clay's interest in Sylvia than in mine. Am I right?"

Avoiding his scrutinizing gaze, she fumbled with her napkin before replacing it in her lap. "I . . . I was only trying to figure out what your reasons were for not telling Sylvia that you and Clay don't want her to have the lead in this new play of yours. That's all I was really asking."

He jerked his head in surprise. "How did you know that?"

"I guessed it from the way both of you were acting that first day, when Sylvia asked you about that pretty song in your new play—the one you and Clay were working on the first time I met you."

"You guessed right. Sylvia is completely wrong for this play—looks, voice, type, everything. She's right for the light, bright, sophisticated musicals Clay's written before. This one is altogether different." Picking up his fork, he began to eat again.

Racile followed suit, wondering if he were trying to get her off the subject of Sylvia or the new play or both. "I know this play is different," she said after they had eaten in silence for several minutes. "Clay told me it was a serious drama with music. Musical theater I believe he called it."

He glanced up from his food and reached for his wine glass. "Is that all he told you about it?"

"I know it's based on notes for an unwritten novel of Trenton Hunter's. That's all I know. I do wish you'd tell me more. I'd love to know what it's about." She spoke quietly, but she inclined her head toward him and raised her chin in a determined angle. "I want you to tell me, Larry."

"It is Clay's play, Racile. He'll have to be the one to tell you."

"Surely he'll tell me now that it's finished. I just hoped you might tell me tonight." She gave him an entreating smile.

"What gave you the idea it was finished?" Larry asked, stern lines bracketing his mouth.

"It must be. Clay told me you were going back to New York in the morning."

"No, it's not. Most of the last act is yet to be written."

He sounded suddenly angry and Racile thought of the conversation she'd overheard earlier. She rubbed her hand across her upper lip, feeling ill at ease and confused by Larry's reactions. "But I guess the music is finished though."

"No, it's not finished either. There will have to be at least one more song. I won't know about that until Clay makes his decision about the ending for the play." Larry's words sounded sharp enough to slice the air.

"Then I don't understand," she said, running her tongue over her dry lips. "Why are you leaving tomorrow, if you still have work to do on the play?"

"Clay and I can't work together right now, Racile, and I really don't want to discuss all the reasons. We don't agree on some aspects of this and I can't say I approve of his method of doing things. He's too intense about this play and he's using everything and everybody in the wrong way and for the wrong reasons. Now let's change the subject and order dessert." With a brooding frown creasing his forehead, he signaled their waiter.

It was late when they started driving back to Briny Bay. The June night was pleasant and overhead the moon soared into the dark blue heaven attended by dozens of stars. Larry kept her talking about her job and the latest designs she had just delivered to her company. By the time they reached the road to Hunter's Ridge, Racile realized that she had been giving Larry what amounted to a soliloquy on her ideas to go along with the trends in wallcoverings for next year.

Larry parked alongside Clay's house and the two of them got out of the jeep. It was evident from the lights glowing inside Clay's house that he was still up working. Because of the friction existing between them, Racile sensed Larry's reluctance to encounter Clay.

"What do you say we don't disturb Clay when he's working?" she said quickly. "And anyway, since I've spent the last half-hour telling you all that I do for a living, it's now your turn. I've a perfectly good, baby grand piano in my living room that needs playing. I intend to be treated to some Larry Vernon originals before we end this evening." Smiling, she put her hand out to him. "Come on."

Larry took hold of her hand, giving it a grateful squeeze. "If you want to hear 'em, I want to play 'em." He tucked her arm through his and they walked across the ridge toward her house.

Entering the house, Racile turned on the lamps in the living room. Walking to the far end of the room, she lifted the lid of the piano and propped it open with the wooden lid brace.

"I think it's in pretty good tune. I tried my own repertoire on it when I first arrived," she said with a self-effacing laugh. "My playing isn't much, but the piano has a lovely tone."

"I'm learning a lot of things about you tonight. You can draw *and* play."

She laughed again. "My designs are good. I'll give myself that. But I can't say as much for my halting rendition of Debussy's "Clair de Lune." She pointed her finger at the piano bench. "You sit down and play while I get us something to drink. I can make coffee or I have some Rhine wine."

"Make mine the wine." He was already trying out the piano and he accompanied his answer with arpeggios.

When Racile came back from the kitchen with their wine, Larry was playing the songs from *Rainbow's End.* "Would you like to hear the new one we wrote for Sylvia this weekend?"

"Sure." She nodded. "It caused such havoc, I would love to hear it."

It was a rhythm and blues tune, the kind Sylvia did so well. She might not have a well-trained voice, but Sylvia Sontag had her own special tricks of inflection and emphasis that were at their best in this type of song. She had proved to be the ultimate star for a Forrest-Vernon musical, at least for the ones they had written so far. Now, listening to this tune written expressly for the vibrant actress, Racile had reason to wonder how Sylvia was going to accept the fact that she was not to have the lead in Clay and Larry's new production?

"I like that. It's the kind of song Sylvia does with her own special flair," she commented, when Larry took his hands from the keyboard long enough to take a drink of his wine.

"It'll do, I guess. I'd hardly call it a showstopper, but it satisfied our prima donna." He made a guttural sound deep in his throat, shrugging indifferently.

"Are you gargling or strangling on the wine?" She got up from the wing chair where she'd been sitting and came over to lean in the curve of the piano. She studied his face, her eyes twinkled with amusement.

"More like laughing at Sylvia. She manipulates everyone, but she does it beautifully." He chuckled, and set his glass down. "Do you know the real reason she wanted this song and why she went to such lengths to get it?"

Racile shook her head, narrowing her eyes curiously. "Why?"

"Well it seems the movie director decided to feature the male lead in one of the ensemble numbers. That meant that Sylvia's co-star now had exactly the same number of songs in the movie as she did. Can't you just picture her reaction to that?" Larry's dark eyes filled with impish glee. "Of course, she didn't rest until she'd convinced the man that the movie needed another song, a new song, naturally one that she would sing."

"Does Clay know this?"

"No way. He'd have put a bullet through her self-centered little heart." He frowned, holding his forehead in his hand. "Poor Clay, he'd planned on completing the lyrics for the title song of the new play this weekend. Stopping that to do lyrics for a tune for Sylvia was enough of a disaster. It really did put him in a foul mood." Larry's hands touched the piano keys again. It was clear to Racile that he was more comfortable playing than talking.

She leaned against the piano and listened. After a few notes, she realized he was playing the beautiful melody which she recalled hearing that first afternoon at Clay's house. Leaning on her elbows, she moved her face closer so she could watch his mobile fingers caress the ivory keys, drawing forth rich, sensuous tones. The melody was lyrical, yet it had a poignant quality that touched a wellspring of emotion within her. For a brief moment as he played, tears sprung to her eyes. When the music ended, she let out a deep sigh.

"That has to be the loveliest piece of music you've ever written."

He looked up, his eyes meeting hers. "It's the title song for Clay's play," he said quietly, then pressed his lips together firmly.

Racile thought he was not going to say anything more and she fully expected him to play some of the other music he'd written for the new play. Instead he put his hands down at his sides, curving them around the edge of the piano bench.

"Do you know what it's called?" There was a ring of determination in his voice. "The play will have the same title as Trenton Hunter had planned for his novel—*Madelaine*."

Racile could almost feel the color drain from her face and she pressed her body hard against the piano for support. Madelaine . . . Madelaine . . . Madelaine, her mother's name reverberated through her mind like an echo bouncing off canyon walls. This then was the piece of the puzzle that once discovered and put in place made all the other pieces fit. A sudden sharp pain tore at her heart. Everything Clay had done had been only because of the play. He had spent time with her, kissed her, held her, and even would have made love to her, all as a means to an end. Clay believed she was Trenton Hunter's Madelaine and so to him she was nothing but a tool. A tool he would merely use and then discard when he no longer needed her.

Taking a long, steady breath to calm herself, she struggled to control the storm of emotions pouring through her. "Whatever the title, I'm certain you and Clay have another hit on your hands." She managed to say the words in an offhand way. At the same time, she turned her back to Larry and moved away from the piano. She tried to think of a tactful way to get Larry to leave.

As if he were able to read her mind, Larry stood up. She heard him remove the prop and lower the lid of the piano. "I'd like nothing better than to sit here and play all night. But if I want to get a morning flight back to New York, I'd better go make my peace with Clay."

She knew from the sound of his voice that he was walking toward her. When she felt his hand touch her shoulder, she turned and walked with him to the front door.

"I think we got to know each other tonight Racile. I'm glad for that." He let his hand slide down her arm, taking hold of her hand.

"Me too." She smiled, but her eyes were round and serious. "I enjoyed our dinner and your music." She paused and looked intently into his face. "I want to thank you for everything."

Larry's brown eyes narrowed imperceptibly. "Don't mention it," he said, letting go of her hand and opening the door.

Closing the door after him, Racile was aware that both of them had meant more than they had actually said.

Chapter Eight

Racile tossed and turned for a long time before
going to sleep. She lay still with her eyes closed
but her mind churned with her thoughts. She
wondered why it hadn't occurred to her that
Trenton Hunter's notes were for a novel about
her mother, Madelaine. Even though he had
intended to write a piece of fiction, still his notes
would surely reveal something of the relationship
that had actually existed between him and her
mother. Now more than ever, she knew she had
to get Clay to let her see the story outline Trenton
had made for his last novel. It could explain so
much and she needed to understand what part the
novelist had played in her mother's life. Had her
mother loved this man? Had her mother been
unhappy with her father, her own husband? If so,
why hadn't she divorced Ned Douglas and mar-

ried Trenton Hunter? Had her mother stayed with her father because of her? Racile turned over on her stomach, burying her head into her pillow. Deep inside she felt the answer. Her mother had always been conscious of her responsibilities and loyalties. She could not have ended her marriage, nor allowed her child to be torn in half by divorce. Had Madelaine ever seen Trenton after that one summer? Had that been the end? And had the novelist waited all those years to write his novel because he had been waiting for a different ending to his love story—a happy ending?

Clay had told her that day on the ferry that he didn't have an ending for his new play, that he didn't know how his father intended his novel to conclude. That was what Larry had meant about Clay using everything and everyone to solve the dilemma of finding a conclusion to his play. She saw it all now. It was achingly clear. She had fallen in love with him, but all he sought from her were answers for his writing. He believed she was Trenton Hunter's Madelaine. And because he did, he was using every possible means to get close to her and know her emotions, her reactions and her capacity for love.

Clay wanted something from her and she wanted something from him. The tragic part was that the two them actually wanted exactly the same thing: to discover and understand the extent of the love affair that must have existed between Trenton Hunter and M.R. Douglas. A shuddering sob shattered the silence of the room ending in bitter laughter. How absurd and senseless it was. If Clay hadn't had such a closed mind from the very beginning about her, and if he hadn't made her so furious with his censuring attitude, she could have explained to him about Madelaine weeks ago. She had never meant to deceive him, but he had made it impossible for her to find the right moment to explain the truth.

On the other hand, from Clay's argument with Larry she realized all too clearly that Clay felt no compunction about deceiving her. Maybe it was vindictive malice, but Clay deserved to have the tables turned on him. She could do that if she played her cards right, she thought.

With a start, she flipped over on her back and sat up in bed. *Playing her cards right*—that was exactly where she should start. Jumping out of bed, she ran barefoot across the hall to the large master bedroom. Switching on the overhead lights, she knelt down in front of the bookshelves, taking three volumes out to retrieve the envelope containing her mother's souvenirs. She removed the fortune card from the envelope before replacing it beneath the row of Trenton Hunter's novels. She was smiling now as she tapped the card lightly against the palm of her hand.

The following morning, she slept later than usual. She did not linger in the shower, but lathered her body quickly with a new bar of French-milled soap in the same scent as her favorite perfume. Rinsing thoroughly first under warm then cold water, she stepped out of the shower and vigorously toweled her body until it was pink and glowing. She dressed in canary-yellow linen weave slacks and a matching yellow

132

and white striped top with a scooped boat neck. She ate her breakfast, taking time for a second cup of coffee before she gathered up her beach hat, sunglasses and a shoulder bag filled with everything she might need while spending the day exploring some of the villages and beaches on the Cape.

Before she left her house, she looked out the window toward Clay's house to make sure the jeep was there. He was back from taking Larry to catch his plane. She had planned her scene carefully, and the audience to whom she wished to play was Clay.

Outside, she got in her car and started the engine. As soon as it caught, she turned it off. She did the same thing twice again, hoping to simulate some problem with the motor. The fourth time when the motor caught, she put it in drive and drove a little more than half the short distance that separated her house from Clay's. Deliberately, she turned the ignition off. She waited a few minutes, sitting hunched over the steering wheel, as if attempting to figure out the trouble, in case Clay might be in his house watching her. Then, she got out and walked the remaining fifty feet to Clay's front porch. Knocking firmly on the frame of the screen, she called loudly through the open door.

"Clay . . . Clay, I need help. I've got a problem with my car." She raised her voice and hollered his name again. "Clay." She wanted to make sure he could hear her if he were working in his study.

"Hold on. I'm coming," he yelled back at her.

A minute later she could see him walking to the door and running his hands through the sides of his hair to smooth it down as he came to meet her.

"I'm sorry to bother you when you're writing." Her innocent smile was intended to make him believe in the sincerity of her words. The truth was, of course, that she wanted to bother him, interrupt his writing and finally find a way to manipulate him into allowing her to see Trenton Hunter's notes. She lowered her lashes to avoid looking into his eyes. "I was all set to go to the beach and I had trouble with my car. The motor catches then dies on me." She threw up her hands in a gesture of bafflement. "I really can't understand. It ran perfectly all the way to Philadelphia and back."

Clay propped a hand on his hip and looked at her thoughtfully. "Probably just a little dirt in your fuel line. Why don't you take my jeep."

"I couldn't do that," she said, a small frown appearing on her brow. "I may be gone all day. I'm even taking cheese and fruit with me for a picnic lunch."

A slow smile eased the lines of Clay's face. "In that case, I think the only thing for me to do is come with you."

"Could you?" she asked innocently, returning his smile. She felt an unexpected feeling of excitement. She hadn't realized how much she wanted to spend another day with him. One at least, somewhat like the day they'd spent at Martha's Vineyard. She rubbed her hand across her chin. She had better proceed with caution; she'd never accomplish her purpose if she let her emotions run away with her like this. "You don't have to do that, Clay." Her face grew sober. "I know you want to spend your day writing. Larry told me last night that you still had most of the last act of your play to complete."

"That's right, I do. But I'd rather take you to Sandy Neck Beach. I will gladly skip a day of writing in order to spend it with you."

She felt a twinge of guilt knowing she'd lied to him about her car. "I . . . I probably have only flooded my engine. Maybe I could make my car run and. . . ."

"If it stalled on you now, it could again. You could get stranded on the beach and I'm not taking a chance on that. I'm taking you and I'm even bringing along a bottle of wine as my contribution to our picnic." His voice was firm and his words dismissed all thought of her going anyplace today alone.

His reaction was exactly what she had hoped for. She had planned to manipulate him into spending the day with her, and he had swallowed the bait. It had all evolved easily, almost too easily. For a moment she wanted to believe Clay wanted to be with her, and that he had grabbed at the excuse to drive her in his jeep because he really cared for her. But, of course, she knew better. For Clay, the day would only be a chance to discover more about her for his play. She stiffened inwardly. And she'd use the time with him to her own ends.

While Clay went to fetch a bottle of wine from the rack in his kitchen, Racile walked back to her car and took out the sack of cheese, crackers and fruit she'd left on the front seat. Clay was putting tin pails and a rake in the back of the jeep when she joined him.

"What's that?" she inquired.

"It's a clam rake. I thought it would be fun to dig some steamer clams when the tide goes out."

He ran around the back of the jeep and opened the door on the passenger side, helping her in. His face was wreathed in a good-humored smile and he was acting as if the entire idea for an outing at the beach had been his idea. He looked suddenly like a high-spirited young boy and she felt her heart leap crazily. She bent her head, busying her hands with fastening her seat belt. She was a fool and it was self-destructive to allow everything about Clay to affect her so deeply.

It took them less than half an hour to drive to Sandy Neck Beach. They left their shoes in the jeep and ran barefoot through the sand to the water's edge. Clay took hold of her hand and they walked along the beach where the tide had advanced and then withdrew, leaving the sand firm and wet and glistening. She caught the tidal smell of the seaweed and heard the terns crying over head. She looked up to watch the birds swoop and dive over the water.

There were only a few people scattered here and there on the beach. Racile was intent on talking to Clay and she scarcely noticed them. She was surprised at how comfortable she felt being with Clay, walking along, holding his hand and telling him inconsequential jokes.

Later, they retraced their steps, returning to

the jeep to pick up the food they had brought for their lunch. Clay then led the way to where the remains of an old wooden barge rested on the sand. Beach grass grew around the old worn planks of the barge, making a secluded spot for their picnic.

Neither of them had thought to bring a knife, so they had to break pieces from the wedge of cheese with their fingers. Racile pealed the skin from the oranges, pulling them apart, offering sections to Clay. As they ate, they took turns drinking wine from the bottle. It was fun and they found themselves laughing and enjoying the carefreeness of their situation.

"I've saved the last for you," Clay said, holding the almost empty green bottle out to her.

Shaking her head, she refused the wine. "I've had more than enough. I don't want to make a bacchanal feast out of this."

"Why not?" He edged closer to where she sat leaning her back against the pile of wood planks. "I think the idea has delightful possibilities." He rubbed his shoulders against hers. Making a little growling sound in his throat, he leaned over and began nuzzling the soft skin of her neck. "Drink my wine, fair lady. Then let me taste the sweetness of your grape-scented lips."

"Idiot." She laughed, pushing him away. She sat up straight and began to close the wax paperlining around the remaining crackers in the paper box. "This *is* a public beach, Clay Forrest. One is not allowed to litter, loiter or indulge in improper conduct on a public beach." She glanced at him askance, still laughing.

Clay stood up and held his hands down to her. "Come on then. Let's find a private place where I can behave as I feel." He took hold of both her hands and with one strong pull he brought her to her feet.

She was standing face to face with him and so close she could feel his warm breath on her face. She was filled with a profound desire to lift her mouth to his and have him kiss her. Trembling, she pressed her lips tightly together trying to control her longing to feel his hands caress her.

Clay studied her face intently, his expression faintly quizzical. "You don't object to that do you?" He let go of her hands, putting both arms around her and holding her firmly against him.

"I . . . I don't object to leaving here," she said, her voice muffled because she had her face pressed into the hollow of his shoulder. "But I really want to find out about a place I've been wondering about." She lifted her head and eased herself slightly away from him.

"What place is this?" He allowed her to put a fraction of space between them, but he still kept his arms around her waist.

"Do you know if there is an amusement park someplace on the Cape? Something with maybe penny arcade-type places and fortune-tellers?"

Clay's eyes shot to hers in a puzzled look. "I'd hardly call that a private place."

"But . . . is there a place like that?"

"Not that I know of." Frowning at her, he dropped his hands from her waist and bent over to gather up the crackers and the wine bottle.

"I found this on a shelf with your father's

novels. I thought it might have come from some park or fair here on Cape Cod." Taking the fortune card from the pocket of her slacks, she handed it to Clay.

"Where did you say you found it?" he asked, looking at it and reading the printed fortune on the front.

"In an envelope in the bookcase in his bedroom. He'd saved it along with a match folder and few other mementos. I thought it could be something that he kept as a reminder, something he wanted to write about in his next novel."

Clay's eyes sparked with interest and he studied the card again. "You could be right at that." He cocked an eyebrow. "I've saved some odd bits of memorabilia myself because I thought I might use it in a scene sometime." Smiling, he handed the card back to her. "You may even have guessed right . . . this did come from a place on the Cape."

"But you said you didn't know of an amusement park here."

"But I know of something else." He slipped an arm around her shoulders. "Come on and I'll tell you about it while we walk back to the car."

He tightened his arm around her shoulders and she slipped her arm around his back as they began to walk away from the old barge debris.

"I do remember hearing that during the summer months, there's a carnival set up down toward the tip of the Cape, close to Provincetown. They put up a ferris wheel and various rides and I'm sure there are game booths. I imagine they have one of those wagon booths with the gypsy figure inside, where you can put your quarter in the slot and get back a fortune card."

"Oh Clay!" Racile stumbled in the sand in her excitement, causing Clay to hold her securely to keep her from falling. "Do you think the carnival is there now? It's the middle of June. It must be there. Oh, if it is, please take me. Could we go? Won't you take me?" She had stopped walking and she leaned against him, her violet eyes imploring.

"Yes, yes and yes." He laughed. "When you look at me like that I'd take you to the ends of the earth." His eyes held hers for a timeless moment, then he bent his head to hers and covered her mouth with his.

Racile felt the soft warmth of his tongue touching her lips, seeking entry into her mouth. She parted her lips in anticipation. Until this moment she hadn't realized how much she had wanted this to happen. Their kiss was long and deep and intimate. She slid her arms up around his neck and clung to him, reveling in the feel of Clay's arms secure and possessive, holding her again. As he continued kissing her with a slow, melting thoroughness, she could feel the passion mounting between them. The pounding of her heart drowned out the sound of the incoming tide, but she shivered as a cold wave of water washed over her bare feet, splashing up over her ankles. Gasping breathlessly, she drew her mouth away from his.

"The ends of the earth will have to come later," she murmured. "For now, I think the carnival is far enough for you to take me."

He cupped her chin, raising her face to his so he could regard her closely. "All right, Racile. But I intend to change your mind. I think you already know that."

A deep thrill went all the way through her at the emotion in Clay's expression. Her mind told her to steel herself against him, but when Clay looked at her the way he was doing now, her every defense seemed to crumble away.

"I know that right now we should go home to the ridge, so I can take a bath and wash off the sand and salt water," she said unevenly, the thudding of her heart making her voice break. "Come on." She pulled away from him. "I intend for you to take me to the carnival *tonight*." She managed these last words in a louder, steadier tone. She held out her hand to him, and at the same time started walking on ahead.

Instead of taking her hand, Clay caught up to her with one long stride and circled her waist with his arm. "And you're the one who called me bossy," he said with a laugh. Pulling her with him, he quickened his step so they were almost running back toward the jeep.

Racile's fingers trembled with excitement as she took her prettiest summer dress from her closet. It was a salmon pink, pima cotton with narrow shoulder straps. Slipping the smooth fabric over her head, she looked at herself in the mirror. She was pleased by her reflection. The bodice of the dress hugged the contours of her supple body and was cut wide and low to just reveal the first soft rise of her round breasts. A narrow belt cinched her small waist and the semi-full skirt was graceful and flattering to her slender figure. A smile curved her lips when she observed that the soft peach color seemed to add to the warm glow of her skin. Quickly, she ran her comb through her hair, smoothing the crown and letting the loose waves frame her face while the softly curling ends lightly brushed the tops of her bare shoulders. Before leaving her bedroom, Racile picked up the wide, tricornered shawl of the same material as her dress. Putting it casually around her, she looped the ends in a soft knot.

She went downstairs to wait for Clay, and paced around the living room, trailing her hand along the edge of the tavern table at the back of the sofa and fingering the stack of Trenton Hunter's novels she had left on the table. She realized she was both excited and apprehensive about viewing the carnival near Provincetown. Mostly, because it was an event that her mother had enjoyed with Trenton Hunter. She found it somewhat frightening, perhaps, to be on the verge of discovering the depth of Madelaine's love for the novelist. She must admit, too, that she was afraid of her own strong feelings for Clay. There was no escaping from the fact that she was in love with him and this made her painfully vulnerable to him.

When Clay arrived, he looked fresh-shaven and impeccable in fawn-colored slacks and a natural-colored silk shirt, open at the throat. Like the very first time she had seen him, she was struck with the matching tawny color of his hair and eyes. Racile understood why one of the New York drama critics had referred to him as the "golden lion playwright of Broadway musicals."

Clay certainly was not indifferent to her attractive appearance; his gaze swept over her in open admiration. "You are beautiful, lady!" he said, putting into words what his eyes were already telling her. "If I were a poet instead of a writer of plays, I'd compare you to a Tropicana rose." He continued to look at her intently, taking in every detail. "I can't tell you the things you do for that dress," he added with a suggestive glance at the revealing neckline.

"And why not?" she countered with a demure smile.

"Because it would make you blush." He let his fingers brush over the creamy softness of her skin as he slowly secured her shawl around her shoulders.

She felt a curious fluttering in the pit of her stomach and a flush of heat now warmed her face. Why must his slightest touch affect her so deeply? She was afraid, afraid of herself and the emotions that swept through her whenever Clay was near to her. She stepped quickly through the door, glad to find that outside the dusk curtained the air in a soft purple twilight. Maybe Clay could not detect her every nuance of emotion in this fading evening light. She felt Clay's hand glide under her elbow, taking hold of her arm with practiced ease.

"I didn't take time to clean the sand out of the jeep, so I thought we could take your car. I looked under the hood just now and I'm certain there will be no more trouble with it."

She wondered if he suspected that she'd made

up the story about car trouble that morning. "My car. . . ." She hesitated, not wanting to give herself away. "It's fine if we take it, but are you sure it will run okay?"

"I'm very sure it will," he said, guiding her toward where she'd left her car between their two houses.

Racile stole a glance at his profile. Though she could see he was not smiling, she thought she detected a trace of amusement in his voice.

Chapter Nine

Clay and Racile ate dinner in an attractive bayside restaurant near Truro and then drove the short distance to the site of the carnival. The June night was ink black due to the curtain of clouds which hid the stars. The carnival grounds, however, glowed brightly beneath a canopy of tinsel strings of colored lights.

They parked the car and walked through the entrance gate above which stretched a white banner lettered in bold, black letters declaring it to be BATES BROTHERS, SEAFRONT CARNIVAL. Inside everything was going at full tilt. The tinkle of a hurdy-gurdy mixed with the reedy sound of the calliope, and as they wandered near the merry-go-round, Racile could distinguish the tune it played. It was "Love Makes The World Go Round," and it played over and over again as the circular platform turned. The sights and sounds absorbed her. She was like a child fascinated, curious and enthralled by the spectacle before her. The paint had long since worn off the prancing steeds, so when Clay lifted her onto one of the wooden horses that moved up and down on its tarnished metal pole, she found it easy to believe her mother could have ridden this same, once shiny, black painted animal. Indeed, she felt this could be the very same carnival Madelaine had enjoyed with Trenton Hunter.

The repetition of the lilting tune and the easy, fluid motion of the merry-go-round filled her with a sensation of déjà vu. Someplace and sometime back in her childhood, she had ridden on a carousel like this one. She wondered if her mother and father had taken her to an amusement park in one of the cities where they had lived. She didn't actually remember, but she felt quite certain that something like that had happened to her. It could have been during that summer she spent with her grandparents. Perhaps they took her to a county fair. There are always rides for children to enjoy at state and county fairs. And it would be exactly like her grandfather to think of taking her there, where she could be entertained with all the rides and eat her fill of spun sugar candy cones, hot dogs and root beer. The thought of that long ago summer filled her with nostalgia, and perhaps a tinge of regret.

Her hands gripped the metal pole more tightly. Would she ever know what really happened to her mother during that summer? What kind of impact had Trenton Hunter and a summer spent on Cape Cod had on the life of Madelaine Douglas? She doubted if she would ever know all about it, but there was one thing she did know: it was because of that period in her mother's life that she was here with Clay. Otherwise she would never have come to Cape Cod at all, let alone be riding a carousel which very likely her mother had ridden on a summer night like this sixteen years ago.

Feeling slightly dizzy, Racile leaned her head against the pole. *Stop the music! I want to get off!* She thought she had cried out the words to Clay. Obviously they had only sounded inside her head for he gave no sign that she had uttered a sound. Clay sat astride a faded brown wooden horse across from her. It was apparent from his smile that he felt she was enjoying herself. He seemed to take pleasure in the thought that she was amused by the carnival festivities.

The platform was spinning slower now, getting ready to stop. "Want to go again?" Clay asked her gaily.

She shook her head. "Going up and down and round and round at the same time is starting to make me feel as if I've had one too many glasses of champagne." Her attempt at a smile resulted in a feeble waver at the corner of her lips.

Clay slid immediately off his mount to stand beside her. Placing his hands under her arms, he lifted her gently down. "You'll be okay when you get your pretty feet back on terra firma." He kept his warm hands firmly against the sides of her breasts as they stood pressed together in the narrow space between the rows of wooden horses.

The merry-go-round had ceased turning but the music continued, still with the same, familiar love song. Racile didn't notice the other riders leaving the platform; she was only conscious of Clay's body touching hers, of the energy that radiated from his body, of his magnetism and his sexual appeal.

She looked at him, her eyes wide and lustrous.

"Racile, don't look at me like that when I can't do anything about it," he whispered hoarsely, letting his hands slide slowly down, shaping her body. There was no mistaking the intensity of his desire for her. It was in his eyes, his hands, in the taut muscles of his body. Her eyes clung to his and she let her breath out in a soundless sigh. He took her hand then and guided her through the space between the wooden figures, now empty of riders. As they stepped down from the carousel together, Clay kept his face angled away so that she couldn't see the emotions marking his expression.

They walked through the center of the carnival, skirting the groups of people who mingled about in front of the various booths which lined the midway. Though Clay still held her hand, he maintained a space between them, so there was no chance of their bodies touching as they walked. Neither of them spoke. They just walked slowly, holding hands, both looking everywhere but at each other.

"Step right up. Toss a ring and win a prize." A hawker began his spiel as they passed a game booth. "It's easy. You can win every time. Hurry, hurry, step this way sir and win a valuable prize for the pretty lady."

Racile hesitated, looking at Clay to see if he was paying any attention to the man's chanting sales pitch. "Let's watch. I think that fellow with the girl in white shorts is going to play."

"All right," he said, without enthusiasm, but he followed her over to the booth. They stood close to the counter, but off to one side to appear as onlookers instead of participants.

The teenage boy Racile had indicated placed several coins on the counter. Taking one of the rings in his hand, he struck a pose that was somewhere in between that of a Roman discus thrower and pitcher of horseshoes. The girl at his side watched him first with admiring eyes and then with unadulterated adulation, when, with his fourth ring, he circled the pin in front of a curly white, stuffed poodle. The girl squealed with excited delight and clutching the furry toy, she snuggled adoringly close to her boyfriend as he put his arm around her shoulders and led her away.

"That has to be the happiest girl and the proudest fellow I think I ever saw." Racile continued watching the couple as they mingled into the stream of people moving along the midway.

"Don't tell me you want one of those idiotic stuffed toys?"

Her eyelashes flickered and she gave him a beguiling smile.

"Don't say it. Don't you even think it, Racile." He scowled, crossing his arms across his chest. "You're not going to get me to stand up there and make a fool of myself pitching hoops in an attempt to win some stupid bit of worthless junk for you."

"Are you afraid, Clay?" she teased. "Scared you couldn't hit anything?"

"I know damn well I couldn't." He grinned. "Furthermore, I'm not some high school show-off who needs to impress my girl with my physical skills in front of a crowd of people." He pulled her away from the counter. "Anyway, I thought you wanted to come to the carnival to get your fortune told." Hugging her close against his side, he synchronized his step to hers and they moved on down the midway. "We'll search every booth here until we find you a gypsy with a crystal ball." He chuckled deep in his throat. "One that will tell you that you are about to succumb to the amorous advances of a brilliant, bossy playwright."

"She won't see that in her crystal ball, Clay," she said tartly.

"No, but she'll see it on the five-dollar bill I lay across her lined palm." He gave her a sly wink.

Racile shook her head, but she couldn't keep from smiling. It was a lovely night and they were having fun together. She didn't want to think of anything beyond the moment. In fact, she would like to prolong this night and their time together for as long as she could. She liked walking close to Clay, her shoulder brushing his arm, the curve of her hip rubbing against the lean hardness of his thigh. His body generated a heat that warmed her and she felt it now like an intimate caress touching the side of her body from her shoulder to her knee. Clay's nearness was exciting, yet at the same time comforting. In her heart, she knew he was the man she wanted to walk beside now, and always.

Near the end of the midway stood a replica of a gypsy wagon. Shiny purple cambric curtains were parted to reveal a small, dark woman methodically spreading a row of cards across a card table in front of her. A multicolored scarf bound her hair and gold loop earrings dangled from her ears.

"I don't see any crystal ball," Clay muttered under his breath. "I wouldn't take much stock in a gypsy who doesn't have a crystal ball to gaze into," his voice was teasing. "Maybe we should pass this up."

"No we won't. This is what I came for." Racile broke away from Clay and hurried forward. As she approached the gypsy, Racile's eyes focused on the cards the woman was handling. Her breath caught in her throat; the cards were the same size and design as the one her mother had kept as a souvenir.

Racile stepped up and stood directly in front of the woman. Clay took his time following after her, pausing to remain a few feet behind as Racile began speaking to the gypsy.

"I'd like to have my fortune told. Could you do it for me now?" she asked.

The fortune-teller had kept her head bent over the table as she dealt out the cards. When Racile spoke to her, she lifted her head slowly, arching her neck and turning her head in a way that made the large brassy earrings swing back and forth like a clock pendulum. She leveled her jet-black eyes on Racile's face, peering at her with a dramatic stare which Racile felt was intended to be hypnotic. The olive-complexioned woman was adept in her role of soothsayer.

"If the fair one will place two dollars in my palm, I shall see what the lines in her hand and the fortune cards reveal." She laid her hand, palm up, on top of the table and waited in silence while Racile complied with her request.

With a sleight of hand movement as skilled as that of a magician, the gypsy whisked the money out of sight. She then asked Racile to take a chair across from her and to place her palms on the table. The light streaming through the arched doorway of the wagon was sufficient to partially illuminate the area around the card table, but now the fortune-teller pulled the beaded cord to turn on a mushroom-shaped lamp at the corner of the table. The cards and Racile's hands were instantly bathed in an amber glow. The diamonds surrounding the emerald in Racile's ring shimmered, the emerald appeared as dark and green as a jungle pool in a rain forest. The older woman eyed the ring with appraising interest.

"You have a strong sentimental attachment to this ring and it fits well upon your slender finger." She paused and leaned forward in her chair, directing her gaze now at Racile's face. "However, you are not the first to wear it."

Racile's eyes flared in amazement. "How could you know that?" Her voice spiraled. Clay moved closer to her chair.

"I know many things, my dear. And some things I *sense*. Your ring belonged to someone else before you. Is this not true?"

Racile continued to stare, her eyes unblinking and her heart pounding so hard it felt as if it might explode. Was it possible? Could this be the same gypsy that her mother and Trenton had seen at the carnival all those years ago? Had this strange, dark woman seen the emerald on Madelaine's hand then, and if so, could she possibly be remembering it now? Racile shuddered. It was entirely unlikely. She was just allowing her imagination to run away with her. Working as a carnival fortune-teller was scarcely a lifetime occupation. Surely, no one, gypsy or not, would continue coming here for fifteen summers or more. This was a small operation and certainly wouldn't make any kind of substantial money. She was being absurd to think for one moment that this woman actually knew anything about the ring. She'd merely tossed out a statement hoping to hit on something that might strike a chord and make her seem to be a psychic. It was a well-known device and it had worked because Racile was in such a romantic and nostalgic mood. Fortunately she was able to let her mind now rationalize her thought processes. Managing to breathe normally, she nodded her head.

"It was my mother's ring. When she died, it came to me," she said softly. Turning her head, she glanced at Clay to see if he was listening. He stood with his feet spread apart in a relaxed stance, his hands on his hips, an expression on his face that could be interpreted either as amused tolerance or veiled skepticism.

Following Racile's gaze, the woman also looked at Clay. "You, sir, I know are interested in the things which concern the lady. There is one thing more to be said about the piece of jewelry that she wears." She interlocked her fingers as she spoke, and resting her chin on her interlaced hands, she looked from Clay back to Racile, indicating that what she had to say was intended for both of them.

"We look at the evergreen trees that remain the same through each season of the year. Their vibrant greenness never fades, never changes. They endure and remain ever green. Likewise, due to its green color, the emerald becomes the symbol of an everlasting emotion. Thus when the gem is given as a gift of love, it signifies an enduring devotion, one that will never lessen, never change, never die." With a significant pause, she lifted her chin from her hands and again looked from Racile to Clay before continuing. "Consider what I've said when you seek answers to the questions that plague your mind and trouble your heart." She looked now at Racile, her eyes softening in a smile.

Racile rubbed her hand across her forehead, bemused by the gypsy's words. It was uncanny that the fortune-teller dwelt on the ring Trenton Hunter had given her mother. It was also weird the way she involved Clay, almost as if she were speaking as much to him as she was to her. Racile shifted uneasily in her chair, wanting suddenly to stand up and end this encounter. Somehow instead of being a frivolous bit of fun, having her fortune told had become a serious act, one she was not enjoying.

As if she sensed Racile's feelings, the woman

turned her attention to the cards she had already spread across the table. Straightening them in to even rows of eight cards each, she began giving instructions to Racile.

"Before you select your card, I must first examine the lines in the palms of your hands. May I please," she extended her own hands invitingly. As Racile put her hands in those of the gypsy, the older woman leaned forward, bending her head to examine the markings in them. "Your life line is strong and unbroken. You will live a long time and in good health." She glanced up for a moment to give Racile a reassuring smile, then lowered her dark eyes again. "There is much uncertainty in your heart. The love you seek eludes you. Perhaps your fortune card will aid you." Withdrawing her hands from beneath Racile's, she pointed to the rows of cards. "Now, take your time, and rub your fingers across the center of each card. One will feel different to you. When you discover it, pick it up, take it away with you."

Racile looked down at the cards, frowning. Touching the cardboard squares was silly, ridiculous hocus-pocus. One slick card would feel exactly like the next. Why was she letting herself be caught up in this sham? She was acting as if she actually believed this woman was something more than a fake gypsy in a mediocre outdoor carnival.

As surely as if she had read her mind, the gypsy fingered one of her gold earrings, giving Racile a knowing smile. "Believe me. You will discover which card is yours. When you find it, there will be no doubt in your mind."

Clay had remained standing an arm's length from Racile's chair, watching everything that took place with a look of mild curiosity on his strong-boned face. He now moved directly behind Racile's chair, so he could observe each movement she made.

Racile touched the first card gingerly, moving the three middle fingers of her right hand over it slowly before moving on to the next. At the sixth card, she touched her fingers to the slick finished paper then instantly drew her hand back. She put her hand to her face, placing it against her lips. Holding her breath, she pressed her suddenly cold fingers hard against her warm trembling mouth. It was unnerving, but it was true. She knew as surely as she had ever known anything before. The card she had just touched was her card. Releasing her breath at the same time as she put her hand down to take up the sixth card from the table, she held it up closer to the light so she could read the printing on the front side. *Find your true happiness among love's souvenirs,* it read. Her fingers shook and the words blurred on the fortune card. She tightened her grasp on the card, willing her hand to hold it straight and steady before her. Reading through the seven pertinent words again, she then looked in wonder at the colorfully-costumed woman opposite her.

"You're right. This is my fortune card," she said in a quiet, confident voice. She was surprised at how calm she sounded. "Thank you," she added, smiling now, because the woman looked suddenly pleased by Racile's words. She put her fortune card inside the small, white clutch purse she carried with her and stood up. She turned to Clay as if to signify she was ready to leave. Before he could take hold of her arm however, Racile turned back to speak to the fortune-teller again. "May I ask you just one question before we go?"

The woman nodded and began to gather up the cards remaining on the table in front of her.

"How many years have you been here at this carnival on the Cape?"

The gypsy began to shuffle the cards, her black eyes narrowed in thought. "I can't recall the exact number, my dear. But I have come here many, many summers indeed. And I shall come again." She bent her head over the card table and began to methodically deal her fortune cards another time, placing them face down in two neat rows. Obviously she did not intend to say anything more. To further indicate that the session was over, the woman paused in her dealing of the cards long enough to pull the beaded cord on the mushroom shaped lamp, extinguishing the glow of amber light.

Clay and Racile started walking back down the midway. "She was rather a strange one. Are all fortune-tellers so bizarre?" Clay asked, taking hold of her hand and measuring his steps to match hers.

"I don't know. I never had my fortune told by a gypsy before. She amazed me. Even frightened me a little, talking about my ring like that." She tightened her fingers around Clay's as she spoke.

"She put on a convincing act. I'll give the old girl that."

"Then you should have let her tell your fortune

157

for you. She might have told you something very interesting about what the future holds for you."

He stopped abruptly and leaned over, putting his mouth close to her ear. "I'm only interested in what the future holds for the two of us." He spoke in a husky whisper, his warm breath teasing the hair at her temple. "Right now I want to have you all to myself, away from merry-go-rounds and carnival barkers. The things I want to say and do need a private place without brassy music and gaudy lights."

Her heart beat quickened. His words were like an intimate touch, sensuous and suggestive. A sweet thrill of excitement quivered down her spine.

"I'm taking you back to the ridge right now." In long vigorous strides, he took off, pulling Racile along with him. She made no effort to protest. She had no desire to. Excitement mounted as she was forced into a run to keep up with him.

When they reached the car, she leaned against it breathlessly. "When you say right now, you mean it," she gasped. "Were you trying to break the record on the quarter-mile dash?"

Clay wrapped his arms around her and pressed her face against his chest. "Don't talk. Just relax and catch your breath," he said, sliding his hands under the scarf around her shoulders and patting her bare back in a gently soothing manner. "I'm sorry if I walked too fast for you, but my patience was giving out. I couldn't wait any longer to feel you in my arms." His hands on her back were strong and possessive, emphasizing his words.

She felt the warmth of his chest heating her face and she could hear the strong, solid beating of his heart and smell the stimulating male scent of him. One of her hands rested against the front of his shirt. Without being conscious of what she was doing, she toyed with the edge of the material where the shirt was unbuttoned at the base of his throat.

Clay held her, caressing her until her breathing slowed and settled into a normal rhythm again. Then, with one hand, he tilted back her head so he could look into her face. For timeless moments their eyes locked in a long, intimate exploration, a silent communication of wordless questioning and answering.

The deep passionate glow in Clay's eyes shook Racile to the very core, causing a sensuous warmth to flow through her. It was wonderful, frightening and exciting all at once. His lips came down on hers with a deep, tender urgency that filled her with an unfamiliar hunger. Her arms went around him and she abandoned all reserve. She couldn't do anything else, didn't want to do anything else, because this was what she wanted. This was what she had been looking forward to all day.

The restraint was gone from his embrace now and he was kissing her hungrily, holding her firmly against him. She clung to him with a yearning that sprang up from unknown depths and it was wonderful and intoxicating for several precious moments, then it faded away and she was filled with an uneasy fear. Clay had never said that he had any real feeling for her. Was his every attention to her just his calculated effort to further the writing of his play about Madelaine? She stiffened in his arms, withdrawing her mouth from his.

"Clay, we have to stop this," she protested.

"Why?" he asked, keeping his arms securely around her, and her body still firmly molded to his. "I've waited all evening for the time I could hold you and touch you like this. I don't want to stop now."

"This is a public place."

"It's not the noisy, glaring midway." He grinned, leaning his face to hers as if he were going to kiss her again.

"It is a lighted parking lot."

He sidled his glance from right to left. "So it is," he said in mock surprise. Slowly and reluctantly he slid his hands down the sides of her body, then released her. Opening the car door, he held it for her to get in. "I want to tell you, Racile, this is merely the end of Scene One. In a Clayton Forrest play, all the important acts have at least two scenes." His eyes danced and his strong mouth curved upward. "I see you and me in scene two, having some of my famous Irish coffee back at Hunter's Ridge. And the action in Scene Two takes up where it left off here at the end of Scene One." His smile became more pronounced, and as he closed the door, he began to whistle the tune from the carousel. He walked around behind the car and climbed in on the driver's side, still whistling.

Racile began to sing the words along with him.

He paused a second and listened to her. "I like that tune. What's the name of it?"

"Love Makes The World Go Round," she said softly.

"I won't argue with that." He covered her hand where it rested on the seat between them for a brief second. Then they drove away from the carnival and headed back to Briny Bay.

Chapter Ten

Racile leaned back against the seat, closing her eyes. She was glad for the companionable silence which now existed between them. Clay seemed content to concentrate all his attention on his driving; she needed time to sort out her emotions. Before this little drama between them progressed any further, she had to decide exactly how far she was willing to allow it to go. So far, she had maintained little, if any, control over her reactions to Clay. She had behaved like a puppet on a string. All Clay had to do was pull the string and she had done whatever he wanted. What had happened to all her earlier resolve to play the same game?

She swallowed hard, feeling as if a lump of despair were lodged in her throat. The truth was that none of this was a game to her. She loved

Clay. And self-destructive as it might be, she longed to tell him how deeply she did love him, how vital and necessary a part of her life he had become. Tears pushed against her closed eyelids, dampening the edges of her lashes. She thought again about what Larry had told her. It still seemed that Clay saw her only as the tool he needed to finish writing his play. But she had to mean more to him than that. He felt desire for her, she knew that. She'd seen it in his eyes, heard it in his voice, felt it in the touch of his hands and in the pressure of his mouth when he had kissed her. These thoughts stirred the passionate needs deep inside her. Suddenly she felt afraid, afraid of herself and of the intensity of her emotions based on a need that she had never known before.

"You've become awfully quiet," Clay said, breaking the silence inside the car. "Have you fallen asleep on me?"

"No, just relaxing and thinking." She leaned forward, reaching toward the dashboard. "I'll turn on the radio and get us some music."

Clay pulled her hand back and held it. "I don't want to listen to music, I want to listen to you. I just remembered that you haven't told me what was on your fortune card."

"You said a gypsy without a crystal ball was a fake, remember?" She shifted her position so she could look at him. "I don't think you'll be interested in my card."

"I asked what your fortune was and I want to know." He glanced over at her and smiled. "Your past, your present and your future all interest me. Don't you know that?"

163

"I know you're a skeptic about my gypsy fortune-teller and you'll make fun of what my card said."

"No, I won't. I promise. So tell me."

Racile didn't answer at once. Sitting with her back pressed into the far corner of her seat, she tried to read the expression on Clay's face in the dim illumination inside the car. "It said that I would find my happiness among love's souvenirs," she said finally in a soft, hesitant voice, as if still uncertain whether she wanted to tell him or not.

"I don't get it." He shot her a quizzical look. "What the heck are love's souvenirs?"

Racile knew he was amused by the thought that she obviously took the fortune card seriously. But, at least, he was trying not to show it. "It's not exactly easy to explain."

"But it does mean something specific to you?" Now he sounded more surprised than amused.

She fingered the knot of her scarf. "It means several specific things to me."

"Then tell me." They had reached Clay's house and he turned off the motor.

"It's kind of complicated. I'll have to explain something before you can understand about the souvenirs." She put her hand on the car door handle. "I'll tell you later," she said quickly, putting him off. "Right now I want to try some of that Irish coffee you promised me."

Rainbow lay curled up on the front door mat, his shaggy head resting on his front paws. He got up and stretched as Clay unlocked the door, then followed the two of them inside. Clay entered ahead of Racile, switching on lights.

"Make yourself at home. I'll go put the coffee on and be right back." He started to leave the living room. "Oh, before I forget, I'd better return these." He turned back and tossed Racile her car keys. "I confiscated your house key. I hope you don't mind?" His mouth moved in a slow smile.

"Why did you do that?" she asked, surprised.

"Why do you think?" He laughed and it was a rich, resonant sound born deep in his throat.

Clay was out of the room before she could offer a comeback. A shiver of excitement raced through her and she could feel her heart beating fast against her breast. She tugged awkwardly at her purse to open it and put her key ring inside. A delicious feeling of pleasure tugged her lips into a smile. Clay had taken her house key and at this moment she found no reason to object to his having it. She wondered if it was the salt air of the Cape that was making her behave so wantonly? The thought caused her to laugh at herself.

Untying her stole, she placed it and her purse at one end of the piano bench and began looking around the room. She'd been in Clay's house only once before and then she hadn't had time to really see what it was like. She walked the length of the room slowly. The furnishings appeared not to be in any particular style, but rather a mixture of different kinds that made up an interesting combination, warm and comfortable and with a distinct personal atmosphere that belonged to a man like

Clay. There was a large, wheat-colored couch, wine-red leather chairs and a fine old ebony desk. A large Bokhara carpet in tan, gold and black lay on the dark polished wood floor. The wall behind the piano was lined with shelves from floor to ceiling, full of books and stacks of sheet music and magazines.

She liked this room and because it held Clay's desk and the piano, she knew instinctively that he used this room to write all of his plays. Clay was writing the new play here and that meant his father's notes would be there on the ebony desk. She could walk to the desk and possibly read some of what Trenton Hunter had written about her mother. Folding her arms across her breasts, she hugged herself, feeling at once apprehensive and chilled. Rubbing her hands briskly over her bare arms, she deliberately turned her back toward the desk, walking determinedly to the piano. She would not snoop.

She pushed her stole and purse to the far end of the bench and sat down at the piano. Riffling through the sheet music spread out on the music rack, she hoped to find some of the score for the new play. Instead, there appeared to be only several songs from *Rainbow's End* and the latest song Larry and Clay had just written for Sylvia. She began to pick out a few of the notes just as Clay came back.

"There'll be about a ten-minute delay while the coffee perks," he said, and coming over to stand behind her, he placed his hands on her bare shoulders.

She continued to play the notes of the new song.

"I'm afraid that's not one of our better songs." He began kneading her shoulders gently. "It's something Sylvia wanted to add to the movie."

"I know. Larry played it for me. It's a good number for Sylvia, she does the blues so well. I think it's a good addition."

"Oh you do, do you?" He laughed, tracing her neck with his warm fingers.

She sighed contentedly. "You're distracting me and I can't read the notes," she said as she played a chord off-key.

He lifted her hair and bent over to kiss her neck where his fingers had been. "I know even better ways than this to distract you." He buried his head in the curve of her neck and at the same time allowed his hands to brush lightly over her back and shoulders, then slide beneath her arms to cover her breasts. The caress of his hands aroused a pulsing desire through her body. His lips began teasing the sensitive skin behind her ear, each tiny movement setting up shock waves that amplified as they traveled along her spinal column.

"Clay." she barely breathed his name. Lifting one hand from the piano keys, she placed it over one of his, not to draw it away from her breast but rather to sustain the intimate pressure of his touch.

"You don't really want to drink Irish coffee now do you?" His voice was rough with emotion.

She shook her head in a barely perceptible gesture.

"Then get out from behind that blasted piano so I can kiss you." He half pulled, half lifted her from the piano bench. Gathering her into his arms, he fitted her body to his so that her softness curved against the muscles of his chest. His mouth touched hers firmly, kissing her with authority.

Racile clung to him, her arms circling his neck. She could feel his tongue now stroking her lips, urging them apart. Then it was warm and probing inside her mouth. His hands began a slow, sensuous ascent on her body, sending tremors of desire racing through her. The wild clamor of her pulse increased as she felt Clay's body trembling against her own and his heart hammering against her breast.

"God, how I want you," he whispered, his mouth sliding passionately down the warm skin of her throat. As his hands brushed the narrow straps of her dress off her shoulders, his lips found the soft warmth of her breasts. "Come to bed with me, darling."

He had never used a term of endearment to her before. Happiness filled her heart. Almost as if her body was responding of its own volition, she found herself cupping his head between her trembling hands, clasping him against her breast in a gesture of loving surrender.

The next instant, he scooped her up, dolllike in his arms, and taking the steps two at a time, he carried her upstairs. She buried her face in the warm hollow of his neck, thinking only of how much she loved him. She wanted to say the words to him, but she waited, wanting him to say something first. He'd called her darling; he wanted to make love to her. He must surely care about her. And now . . . soon . . . he must surely tell her that he cared.

Clay tugged at the zipper at the back of her dress as he carried her into the shadowed bedroom. Only a pale stream of light filtered into the room from the illuminated hallway. Sinking down on the bed beside her he bent over her, his eyes and fingers and lips caressing her as he undressed her.

"Your skin is like satin," he whispered, as his fingers trailed down her throat, brushing the wispy lace covering from the high perfect curves of her breasts. "You're even more perfect and beautiful than I imagined." His eyes moved over her with such open approval that she trembled and closed her eyes, feeling now both shy and nervous.

Clay touched her face tenderly and brushed his fingers through the edges of her hair. As if he sensed her tension and wished to ease it for her, he touched her temples, rubbing them gently with his fingertips.

"Unbutton my shirt for me," he said still gently massaging her temples.

"What?" Her eyes fluttered open and she gazed up at him, her eyes full of sweet languor.

"Undo the buttons so I can take off my shirt," he said, smiling down at her. "I want to do much more than just look at your lovely body. I want to be able to feel your soft skin against mine." He watched her now through half-closed eyes. As she unfastened his shirt, he traced her cheeks gently with his fingertips and outlined the shape of her lips with his thumb.

Racile ran her hands across his chest, guiding the smooth material off his broad shoulders. His skin was firm, warm to her touch. She liked the strong, male feel of him and she didn't take her hands away, but let them remain, her palms resting in the hollow of his shoulders. A soft growl rose from deep in Clay's throat and he shrugged his shirt off, tossing it to one side of the bed.

Racile lay very still, her heart beating in a wild irregular rhythm, her eyes locked by his. He bent over her, close, so very close, yet not touching his body to hers. She kept looking at him and all she wanted was for him to hold her to him, tell her he loved her. The longing she felt was like a pain that filled her, and nothing could still that pain except the words she wanted to hear Clay say.

He moved his hands along her silken skin and he was looking at her through eyes narrowed with desire. She was trembling now, waiting, feeling the intangible currents flowing between them as the silence stretched. His hands were doing wonderful things to her, making her heart beat faster and faster. The wild clamor of her pulse increased as she saw the harsh light of desire flame in his look that seared her face. She sighed, her eyes clouding with answering passion.

"Oh, Clay," she murmured. "There's something I must tell you. I . . . I want to. . . ."

He stopped her words with his lips, kissing her with a sudden, insistence. "I want too," he whispered urgently. "I want to kiss and touch and know every warm, beautiful part of you. You've put your spell on me Madelaine Racile Douglas." He teased the corners of her lips with feather like kisses. "I want to explore and discover all the reasons you enchant me so."

Her eyes widened and a strangled cry came from deep in her throat. "You called me Madelaine. Why?"

He looked startled. "What do you mean, why?"

"You've never called me that before. I . . . I want to know why you're doing it now? Now when we're together like this." Her voice shook and she had trouble pushing the words out through her trembling lips.

He caressed her shoulders in a soothing gesture. "Surely, you don't mind?" His eyes betrayed a teasing smile. "After all, it is your name."

"No . . . oh no!" Her body shook with a convulsive sob. "It's your play. It's never been anything else, has it? You don't care about me at all. You only want to make love to me so you can discover the ending for your play about Madelaine."

The color drained from Clay's face and his eyes grayed in a look that was a mixture of agony and anger. "How did you find out what the play was about?" The rigid set of his jaw caused a nerve to twitch in his cheek. "Did Larry tell you?"

"I was on the porch last night. I overheard the two of you arguing." She hesitated, not wanting to implicate Larry in this.

"And the virtuous Larry was in such a fit of righteous indignation because I hadn't told you every last detail of the play, that I bet he couldn't wait to fill you in over dinner." Clay spoke bitterly. The hands that had gently caressed her only minutes before, now bit into the soft flesh of Racile's shoulders as he held her away from him and stared into her pain-pinched face.

Attempting to shield herself, she covered her breasts with her hands and arms. "You're wrong about Larry. In fact, it was just the opposite. I did ask him to tell me about the play, but he said I should ask you. He said it was your play and you should be the one to tell me what it was about." She pulled away from his grasp and reached over to recover her clothes. "He did play the title song for me. When he said it was Madelaine . . . well, then I knew, of course."

"After Larry told you that, why didn't you ask me? My God, Racile, we've been together all day, first at the beach and then at the carnival. Why didn't you ask me about it then?"

"Be . . . because," her voice faltered, but she lifted her chin and looked straight into his face, challenging him with her troubled eyes. "I wanted you to tell me yourself. I didn't want to believe you were just using me."

Abruptly, his expression became fierce, his eyes stony. "That's not the reason and you know it. You were incensed to find out my play was about the love affair between you and my father and you furthered this scene between us tonight to get even with me."

His words fanned her anger into high flame.

172

"You're blind and you've closed your eyes, your mind and your heart to everything in your life but this play. Furthermore, what right do you have to hurl accusations at me? Did you want me tonight or did you want information for your play?"

The firm line of his jaw hardened further. "It doesn't matter, does it? I was unsuccessful on both scores anyway." He shrugged and stood up.

"No, only one," she said, lowering her head as she fought to hold back her tears.

"Oh?" He grabbed up his shirt from the side of the bed, thrusting his arms into the sleeves. "What the devil do you mean, only one?"

Racile had her dress back on and was struggling with the zipper. "I'll strike a bargain with you."

Hands planted on his hips, he frowned at her. "I'm in no mood for jokes Racile."

"Neither am I, so listen to me." She flung out her hand, her expression sober, entreating. "You give me what I want and I'll tell you everything you want to know about Trenton Hunter's Madelaine."

Clay's eyes flashed curiously. "What have I to give you? I have nothing that you want . . . unless. . . ." His lips curled in contempt. "Why you clever, scheming vixen. And you had the nerve to accuse me of using you. Trenton's house isn't enough for you. That's it, isn't it? You've been angling all the time to get the rest of Hunter's Ridge from me."

Racile was pressing her lips together so tightly they whitened. She slid off the bed and stood facing him, her hands smoothing the skirt of her dress. "No, it's not that. And you can spare me your bitter insults," she said with quiet dignity. "As I said, I'll answer all your questions, but first I want to see all of the notes Trenton wrote for the novel he planned." She turned and began to walk slowly out of the bedroom. "If you'll get them for me now, I'll leave you and your house alone. I'll go home to the part of Hunter's Ridge that belongs to me." Without looking back to see if he were following her, she went into the hall and headed downstairs. She prayed that she would be able to hide all the hurt and humiliation she was suffering from Clay.

Chapter Eleven

By the time Racile had gathered up her things from the piano bench where she'd left them, Clay was at the ebony desk placing some loose manuscript pages along with a spiral notebook into a manila folder.

She approached the desk. "I'm leaving," she said evenly.

"I'll walk you over." His tone matched hers.

"That's not necessary, but you'd better give me back my door key." She didn't look at him, pretending to be concerned with wrapping her scarf around her shoulders.

Clay stepped directly in front of her and taking the ends of her scarf in his hands, looped them together like he had done at the beginning of the evening.

She stood stiffly, flinching inwardly. "I can do that."

He smiled wryly. "I won't touch you, if that's what you're afraid of." He continued knotting the ends, then lay them against the front of her dress with exaggerated care so that his fingers just barely skimmed over the bare skin of her throat, almost, but yet not, quite touching her.

Breathing raggedly, she stepped away from him.

Clay's eyes searched her face, his expression inscrutable. The tension between them was charged with emotion. He opened his mouth as if he were going to say something to her, then simply shrugged and turned back to face his desk. Quickly, he picked up the manila folder and tucked it under one arm.

"I'll take you home now, Racile."

Touching her elbow with the merest pressure, Clay walked beside her the short distance that separated their two houses. Clay unlocked the front door for her, but when she put out her hand to take the key from him, he put it back in his pocket and shook his head. "You can have your key when I take back Trenton's notes in the morning and we complete our bargain," he said and with no further words, he turned his back and stalked off.

Racile went inside and closed the door wanting only to hide in the seclusion of her own house. What a fool she'd been to cling so to the hope that Clay might really care for her. He cared for nothing but his play. Larry was right. Clay was obsessed with the idea that through the writing of this play he could somehow, at long last, form a bond with his father. He'd duped her. She churned with pain and frustration over all that had happened between them that night. Clay was more than a playwright, he was an actor as well. Certainly he'd acted the part of a lover with skill. He'd aroused feelings and desires in her that she had never felt before, and he'd done it with feigned tenderness and pretended passion. A bitter laugh made her lips tremble and her hands became fists that she pressed against her teary eyes.

Eager as she was to read through the notes Clay had given her, she knew her emotional state was not prepared to handle it right at this moment. She carried the manila folder upstairs with her, placing it on the lamp table next to her bed. When she had undressed, she took a fresh nightgown from the bureau drawer and headed for the bathroom to take a shower.

Turning the taps on full force, she welcomed the pelting spray of warm water, praying that it could somehow wash away the memory of Clay's hands caressing her body. Grabbing a bar of soap, she began to lather every inch of her skin. If she could obliterate every trace of Clay's touch from the outside of her body, maybe in time she could discover a way to obliterate him from her heart.

Twenty minutes later, she sat propped up in her bed, surrounded by a halo of clear light from the reading light by her bed. Opening the spiral notebook that contained Trenton Hunter's notes, she began to read.

As she read, Racile saw a beautiful girl with

golden bronze hair and deep blue-violet eyes moving through days of unequaled joy, experiencing the fulfillment of a perfect love affair. A radiant, vivid creature who was adored by a talented, gifted man. Was this her mother? It hardly seemed possible. Certainly this rhapsodic creature bore no resemblance to the Madelaine who had been Ned Douglas' wife.

She turned the pages of Trenton's notebook with avid curiosity, her eyes grabbing at the words, her mind attempting to absorb and understand how it could have happened. It was incredible and fascinating. In a way, it was like the unfolding of a fairy tale. A once-upon-a-time kind of story that happened in another place and time. Nowhere in the notes had she read that this love affair happened in a summer, years and years ago. It could have been this year or last from all Trenton wrote about it. She looked up from the page and frowned. Now she understood why Clay had thought all the time that she was the girl his father had been involved with. Absently, she pushed her hand through her hair. If only she had told Clay that first morning on the telephone that the Briny Bay house was deeded to her mother instead of to her. Would it have made any difference? Her breasts rose and fell as she sighed deeply. Probably not. He'd still be interested only in his play. All he'd ever want from her was the little information she could offer about how his father came to be involved with Madelaine.

Well, tomorrow she would tell Clay what she'd discovered about her mother and Trenton Hunter. She'd explain about the souvenirs that Madelaine had kept. She'd tell him that from these pieces of paper, the receipt for the engraving of the ring, the ferry ticket, that she'd discovered that two people chanced to meet at a period in their lives when they both must have been lonely and vulnerable. They shared a brief summer affair, a memorable interlude that was set apart from the rest of their lives. And if he wanted to know how it really ended, she believed she could tell him that too. Because in a way it never ended, not for either of them. Their love for each other became a memory that lasted for the rest of their lives.

Closing the notebook she put it on the nightstand and turned off the light. As she adjusted her pillow for sleeping, sliding down in the bed, she felt her tears running down her cheeks like warm rain. She didn't know if she was crying for her mother or for herself. But in time her silent weeping provided release for her pent-up emotions, and she fell asleep.

When she awakened, the pale opal light of morning was filtering through her bedroom windows. She was reluctant to get up and leave the sanctuary of her own bedroom, but she'd made a bargain with Clay and she'd have to carry through with it.

Dreading the telltale marks her emotional tears of the previous night had left on her eyes and face, she avoided looking at her reflection in the mirror while she dressed in a pair of biscuit-brown slacks and an eggshell, button-down collar shirt. In the bathroom, she brushed her teeth and didn't look in the mirror until after she'd splashed her face repeatedly with cold water. This invigorating action left her cheeks glowing, but did not erase the gray shadows that circled her eyes. She applied makeup lightly, using a tawny blusher and a sunny coral lipstick. The results met with her approval. She did not want Clay to know how deeply he'd hurt her last night. She preferred not to give him the satisfaction of knowing what a love-sick fool she was, and that she'd made the self-destructive error of loving a man who cared little or nothing for her.

Halfway down the stairs, she stopped abruptly, turning her head from side to side, sniffing the air. What was that odor? Her puzzled frown changed to surprised disbelief. She smelled bacon cooking and she thought she even detected the aroma of fresh coffee. Her heart thumped hard against her ribs, taking her breath away. It had to be Clay. But what would he be doing in her kitchen at quarter after seven in the morning? Why . . . this morning? Clutching the stair rail with cold fingers, she steadied herself. Damn him, she thought. He couldn't wait to find out what he wanted to know for his play. He could hardly let the sun come up before he dashed over here to give her the third degree about Madelaine. She gritted her teeth, suppressing the hysterical urge she felt to scream. Then, with a decisive toss of her head up, she stormed down the remaining stairs and marched into the kitchen.

"Well, good morning." She paused in the doorway studying the chiseled angles of Clay's profile as he stood at the stove turning strips of bacon in an iron skillet.

He turned his head to look toward her. "It has the possibility of being a good morning. I, for one, want it to be." Only a brief smile eased the tense lines of his mouth and his eyes held a strange moody look.

"I smelled the coffee and bacon as I came downstairs," she said. She felt uncomfortable in his presence, and at a loss to know how to respond to his cryptic remarks. "Smells good."

Clay walked over to where the coffee pot was plugged into a wall socket. "Sit down and drink some coffee while I cook your breakfast." He poured a cup of coffee for her and set it on the kitchen table. "That is if you like bacon and scrambled eggs?"

"Yes, I do. That would be fine." She sat down as he'd suggested, wondering what he was up to, but determined not to ask questions. He had set the stage for some reason known only to him and since he was the playwright here, she'd go along with his little scene.

"Did you sleep well Racile?"

The look of speculation and curiosity in his eyes unsettled her.

"Fairly well. How about you?"

He continued to look at her as he pulled out her chair, waiting for her to sit down at the table. "I didn't sleep," he stated flatly.

She drew in her breath sharply. Had she imagined it or was there a tormented look in the implacable way he gazed at her? Sitting down quickly, she picked up the coffee cup in front of her, raising it to her lips with an unsteady hand.

Clay walked over to the counter and began breaking eggs into a glass, mixing bowl. "I didn't have time to sleep. I had too many things on my mind that I needed to think about."

As he bent his head over the bowl of eggs and began whipping them lightly with a fork, Racile studied the gauntness in his rugged face. He appeared more than just tired. Lines of strain bracketed his mouth. Had what happened between them last night caused him to suffer too? Her hand curled around the cup and she took another sip of the hot liquid. She felt a curious fluttering in the pit of her stomach and a sudden sensation of warmth that she knew was not caused by the coffee.

"I read all of Trenton's notes before I went to sleep," she said, raising her voice slightly as if she were afraid he wouldn't hear her over the sound of his egg beating. "What he'd written gave me a lot to think about too." She hesitated. "Clay. . . ." She set her cup down and laced her hands together. "There's something important that I have to explain to you. Something I should . . ."

"No!" He stopped her, hurling out the word like a sharp command. "I don't want you to explain anything to me yet. We'll have breakfast first." He grabbed up the bowl and carried it over to the stove. "It's very important to me that we take things in order here this morning. And I have something that I must say to you before we talk about my father and you."

Racile was taken back by his words, baffled as well as angered by his attitude. *Important to him!* Well what about the things that *were* important to her? Why was it that every time she started to tell him about Madelaine, he cut her off? She glared at him in fury, wanting to lash out at him and tell him she'd had more than enough of his bossy rudeness. So, everything had to be said and done, when and how he dictated, did it? So be it. The way she felt at this moment, she wondered why she should bother at all to explain about her mother to him. It wasn't going to change anything. She doubted if it even mattered to Clay who Madelaine really was. To Clay, Madelaine was his play. She existed for him solely within the framework of the acts and scenes he'd written.

Without comment Racile got up and busied herself setting the table with silverware and plates. And while Clay scrambled the eggs, she put two slices of bread in the toaster. Her emotions were keyed to a high pitch, but she kept a tight rein on them. If Clay wasn't interested in hearing her explanations, in knowing her feelings, then she'd spare him all talk.

Clay served the bacon and eggs and Racile buttered the toast, putting a piece on each plate. As they ate, Clay kept glancing at her and from time to time even smiling pleasantly. She guessed he was waiting to hear her reaction to the breakfast he'd cooked for her. Still feeling peevish, she said nothing.

"Tastes great, huh?" he finally asked, arching one eyebrow.

"Okay," she nodded.

"Okay is hardly an endorsement of my culinary skills." He looked disappointed.

She ignored the look, and kept on eating.

"At least you're eating my cooking as if it tastes good to you. Either that or you're so hungry this morning you'd eat anything." He laughed.

"It's a very good breakfast, Clay." She put down her fork and lifted her cup. "But do you mind telling me now, why you went to all the trouble to come over here and do this?"

He put his hand on her arm, preventing her from lifting the cup to her lips. "I didn't let you drink Irish coffee last night, so I thought I'd substitute a wake-up cup this morning." He rubbed his hand down her arm, gently forcing her to set her cup back in its saucer. When her hand was free, he took it, clasping it firmly in his. Her pulse thudded in her ear. It was absurd that Clay's every touch affected her. Now with his strong, warm hand holding hers, she enjoyed the feeling of being linked to him for these few brief moments as they talked about mundane things like coffee and breakfast.

"Is that why you kept my key last night? So you could let yourself in this morning and cook breakfast?"

He brought his head close to hers. "I doubt that's exactly what I had in mind, at the time." His lips grazed her cheek as he spoke.

Trembling, she moved her head away from him. "Let me get us some more coffee," she said unevenly, making a feeble effort to ease her hand from his.

"I don't want anymore coffee, Racile. What I want now is to talk to you." His voice deepened and his eyes were no longer smiling but shadowed and intent.

Pushing back her chair, she jumped up. "I want another cup. I like my coffee really hot, and what's left of this has gotten cold."

She flung herself away from him. A kind of panic had taken hold of her and everything that Clay was saying and doing was making her more unsure of herself. She felt as brittle as a piece of old porcelain and as fragile. She knew that if he touched her again she would lose the last remnant of control she had over her emotions. "Better still," she chattered on nervously, "you pour it for me and I'll run upstairs and get the notes, since you're ready now to discuss the play."

Clay leaped from his chair, grabbing her in his arms with such force that he knocked the breath out of her. "Damn it, Racile. It's not the play I want to talk about. And I don't want to talk about what happened in the past between you and my father either. To hell with the past," he swore vehemently. "Don't you know that I spent the entire night, last night, coming to terms with my feelings for you." His eyes blazed furiously down into hers. "And I finally admitted something to myself that I should have known from that day on the ferry to Martha's Vineyard. I love you! I love you and I don't care about anything else but finding the way to make you love me in return. You're going to belong to me, because I intend to marry you," he said fiercely.

She stared at him in open-mouthed amazement, unable to believe he could actually be saying what her ears were hearing. "Oh Clay . . . Clay," she cried, her eyes glistening with happy tears. "I wanted you to love me so much." Her voice broke as she caught her breath in joyous excitement. "And I already do love you. Darling, I think I must have loved you almost from the beginning." She reached up and touched the deep lines etched beside his mouth, wanting to erase them with her words and her touch.

He cupped her head with one hand and his mouth drove down on hers, kissing her with a hungry urgency that equaled, but couldn't surpass, her own. They kissed and held tightly to each other, as though each of them needed the other desperately and more than anything on earth.

Racile clung to him for a breathless eternity. All of her senses caught up in the profound joy of being loved by Clay. Finally, she drew her face away from his.

"I have something I have to tell you." She put her hands against his chest, pushing gently back from the intimate contact of his body.

"Later," he muttered, his hands sliding from her waist to her hip to draw her back against him.

"No, now, Clay." She laid three fingers lightly across his lips to keep him from interrupting. "You have to hear what I want to tell you."

"And you call me bossy." He said the words against her fingers and then kissed them.

"You remember that the gypsy fortune-teller told me that I'd find my happiness among love's souvenirs. She was right and I know what souvenirs she meant."

He nibbled at her fingers so she'd move her hand from his mouth. "I didn't stop kissing you to hear about that fake gypsy," he grimaced. "What do you say we make love now and talk later?"

"You have to listen to me now. It's important." She let her hand rest now at the side of his neck. "Upstairs, there is an envelope with some souvenirs in it that were collected during one summer here on the Cape. They belong to Madelaine," she said and her voice faltered for a second. "The Madelaine who shared that summer with your father."

Clay's hands fell away from her. "Stop it! I don't want you to explain. It's all in the past."

"Exactly! The past! That's what I've tried—over and over again—to tell you. You never let me. You always put me off. But this time, you have to listen. You have to understand." Her voice rose with the intensity of her words. "I told you when we first met, Clay, that I'd never been to Cape Cod before. Don't you see? The souvenirs prove that what happened between Trenton and Madelaine, happened here at Briny Bay."

"My God, what are you saying?" He gaped at her in stunned surprise, the color draining from his face.

"I'm telling you that there was another Madelaine Racile Douglas before me. My mother." She choked on the words as a sob rose in her throat. "Mother was the one who loved Trenton. And he gave her this house because he loved her." She held out her hand to him. "And he gave her this emerald ring," she said, warm tears brimming her eyes. "Like the gypsy said. It's a symbol of an everlasting love."

In sudden comprehension, Clay smiled, erasing the grim lines that had bracketed his mouth. "And you darling, are the other Madelaine Racile Douglas. The one I love, the one who loves me." He caught both of her hands in his, looking at her with fire and joy and excitement filling his eyes. "I can't give you the house or the emerald ring, because they're already yours. But darling, I can give you a love that will never lessen, never change and never die." He pulled her close and suddenly he was laughing.

"I was dead wrong, wasn't I? Never should have called that gypsy fortune-teller a fake."

"Well, it was because she didn't have a crystal ball." Racile excused him with a smile that made her tears vanish. "You said no one could predict what was going to happen without a crystal ball."

"I was wrong about that too," he said, swinging her up into his arms. "I can predict right now exactly what is going to happen between you and me, and I don't need a crystal ball to do it." There was the sound of love in his voice and the look of desire in his eyes. Holding her securely in his arms, he strode out of the kitchen toward the stairs.

Racile could feel joy and happiness spreading around her and through her. A soft, sensuous laugh parted her lips and her hands caressed his strong neck. "Oh, Clay," she said. "You don't even need a gypsy!"

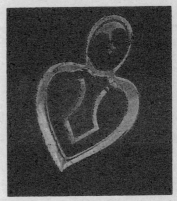

Silhouette Romance

IT'S YOUR OWN SPECIAL TIME

Contemporary romances for today's women.
Each month, six very special love stories will be yours
from SILHOUETTE.

$1.75 each

☐ 100 Stanford	☐ 128 Hampson	☐ 157 Vitek	☐ 184 Hardy
☐ 101 Hardy	☐ 129 Converse	☐ 158 Reynolds	☐ 185 Hampson
☐ 102 Hastings	☐ 130 Hardy	☐ 159 Tracy	☐ 186 Howard
☐ 103 Cork	☐ 131 Stanford	☐ 160 Hampson	☐ 187 Scott
☐ 104 Vitek	☐ 132 Wisdom	☐ 161 Trent	☐ 188 Cork
☐ 105 Eden	☐ 133 Rowe	☐ 162 Ashby	☐ 189 Stephens
☐ 106 Dailey	☐ 134 Charles	☐ 163 Roberts	☐ 190 Hampson
☐ 107 Bright	☐ 135 Logan	☐ 164 Browning	☐ 191 Browning
☐ 108 Hampson	☐ 136 Hampson	☐ 165 Young	☐ 192 John
☐ 109 Vernon	☐ 137 Hunter	☐ 166 Wisdom	☐ 193 Trent
☐ 110 Trent	☐ 138 Wilson	☐ 167 Hunter	☐ 194 Barry
☐ 111 South	☐ 139 Vitek	☐ 168 Carr	☐ 195 Dailey
☐ 112 Stanford	☐ 140 Erskine	☐ 169 Scott	☐ 196 Hampson
☐ 113 Browning	☐ 142 Browning	☐ 170 Ripy	☐ 197 Summers
☐ 114 Michaels	☐ 143 Roberts	☐ 171 Hill	☐ 198 Hunter
☐ 115 John	☐ 144 Goforth	☐ 172 Browning	☐ 199 Roberts
☐ 116 Lindley	☐ 145 Hope	☐ 173 Camp	☐ 200 Lloyd
☐ 117 Scott	☐ 146 Michaels	☐ 174 Sinclair	☐ 201 Starr
☐ 118 Dailey	☐ 147 Hampson	☐ 175 Jarrett	☐ 202 Hampson
☐ 119 Hampson	☐ 148 Cork	☐ 176 Vitek	☐ 203 Browning
☐ 120 Carroll	☐ 149 Saunders	☐ 177 Dailey	☐ 204 Carroll
☐ 121 Langan	☐ 150 Major	☐ 178 Hampson	☐ 205 Maxam
☐ 122 Scofield	☐ 151 Hampson	☐ 179 Beckman	☐ 206 Manning
☐ 123 Sinclair	☐ 152 Halston	☐ 180 Roberts	☐ 207 Windham
☐ 124 Beckman	☐ 153 Dailey	☐ 181 Terrill	
☐ 125 Bright	☐ 154 Beckman	☐ 182 Clay	
☐ 126 St. George	☐ 155 Hampson	☐ 183 Stanley	
☐ 127 Roberts	☐ 156 Sawyer		

Silhouette Romance

IT'S YOUR OWN SPECIAL TIME

Contemporary romances for today's women.
Each month, six very special love stories will be yours
from SILHOUETTE. Look for them wherever books are sold
or order now from the coupon below.

$1.95 each

☐ 208 Halston	☐ 222 Carroll	☐ 236 Maxam	☐ 250 Hampson
☐ 209 LaDame	☐ 223 Summers	☐ 237 Wilson	☐ 251 Wilson
☐ 210 Eden	☐ 224 Langan	☐ 238 Cork	☐ 252 Roberts
☐ 211 Walters	☐ 225 St. George	☐ 239 McKay	☐ 253 James
☐ 212 Young	☐ 226 Hampson	☐ 240 Hunter	☐ 254 Palmer
☐ 213 Dailey	☐ 227 Beckman	☐ 241 Wisdom	☐ 255 Smith
☐ 214 Hampson	☐ 228 King	☐ 242 Brooke	☐ 256 Hampson
☐ 215 Roberts	☐ 229 Thornton	☐ 243 Saunders	☐ 257 Hunter
☐ 216 Saunders	☐ 230 Stevens	☐ 244 Sinclair	☐ 258 Ashby
☐ 217 Vitek	☐ 231 Dailey	☐ 245 Trent	☐ 259 English
☐ 218 Hunter	☐ 232 Hampson	☐ 246 Carroll	☐ 260 Martin
☐ 219 Cork	☐ 233 Vernon	☐ 247 Halldorson	☐ 261 Saunders
☐ 220 Hampson	☐ 234 Smith	☐ 248 St. George	
☐ 221 Browning	☐ 235 James	☐ 249 Scofield	

___#262 WINDOW TO HAPPINESS, John

___#263 SOUVENIRS, Wilson

___#264 ALPINE IDYLL, Vine

___#265 I'LL FLY THE FLAGS, Adams

___#266 HUNTER'S MOON, Trent

___#267 SHARE THE DREAM, Chase

SILHOUETTE BOOKS, Department SB/1

1230 Avenue of the Americas
New York, NY 10020

Please send me the books I have checked above. I am enclosing $_____
(please add 75¢ to cover postage and handling. NYS and NYC residents please
add appropriate sales tax). Send check or money order—no cash or C.O.D.'s
please. Allow six weeks for delivery.

NAME _____

ADDRESS _____

CITY _____ STATE/ZIF _____

READERS' COMMENTS ON SILHOUETTE ROMANCES:

"I would like to congratulate you on the most wonderful books I've had the pleasure of reading. They are a tremendous joy to those of us who have yet to meet the man of our dreams. From reading your books I quite truly believe that he will some-day appear before me like a prince!"

—L.L.*, Hollandale, MS

"Your books are great, wholesome fiction, always with an upbeat, happy ending. Thank you."

—M.D., Massena, NY

"My boyfriend always teases me about Silhouette Books. He asks me, how's my love life and natu-rally I say terrific, but I tell him that there is always room for a little more romance from Sil-houette."

—F.N., Ontario, Canada

"I would like to sincerely express my gratitude to you and your staff for bringing the pleasure of your publications to my attention. Your books are well written, mature and very contemporary."

—D.D., Staten Island, NY

*names available on request